CW00509664

Zainab

The Precious Quest

SHAYAN

Dearest T. Dada / Deb-D
To the coolest couple ever!
Hope you both read it to each other!
With best wishes

Sriontow Basu

6 November 2022
London

Copyright © 2022 by Shayan

ALL RIGHTS RESERVED

No part of this publication may be reproduced, stored in or transmitted, in any form or by any means (electronically, mechanical, photocopying, recording or otherwise), without the prior written permission of both the copyright owner and the publisher of this book.

Re-selling through electronic outlets (including Amazon, Barnes and Nobles, E-bay or any such other distribution channels at present or in the future) without permission of the publisher is illegal and punishable by law.

The scanning, uploading and distribution of this book via the Internet or via any other means without the permission of the publisher is illegal and punishable by law.

Please purchase only authorized editions and do not participate in or encourage electronic piracy of copyrightable materials.

Your support of the author's right is appreciated.

This is entirely a work of fiction and any resemblance to any person or organisation is entirely coincidental. No proprietary or confidential information obtained in the course of any profession or trade has been used by the author.

Bööks by Shayan

Seven Attempts

*To Babbam and Mummum - to whom
I owe everything!*

Contents

Prologue

5 September 1970

Prime Minister Indira Gandhi introduced a law to stop her government from paying an honourary salary or privy purses to 550 royal families who had merged their princely states with the Union of India in 1947. Clearly, the Union of India paying out monies under a constitutional promise to royal families for doing nothing was in conflict with the larger vote bank of Prime Minister Gandhi. This move was struck down by the Supreme Court of India as being against constitutional tenets. In retaliation, Mrs. Gandhi dissolved the Parliament and called for early elections.

5 March 1971

Mrs. Gandhi stormed back to power with a brute parliamentary majority riding on her "*Garibi Hatao*" mantra which brought significant hope to a malnourished and mal-resourced electorate for a more egalitarian social order.

28 December 1971

Mrs. Indira Gandhi successfully engineered the passage of the laws for abolishing the privy purses of the royal families and in one stroke rendered ineffectual a constitutional promise.

6 December 1992

The Babri Masjid in Ayodhya was pulled down by a rabid mob of Hindu right - wing activists which forever wrecked the harmonious co-existence of Hindus and Muslims in Uttar Pradesh and further afield at the altar of petty electoral politics.

17 November 1995

A series of mysterious donations from Saudi Arabia-returned industrial workers in Moradabad, Meerut and Amroha suddenly changed the discourse of Salafism in western Uttar Pradesh. A new muscular and well - funded response to majoritarian acts of the past decade was being prepared in seminaries along this belt.

4 February 2002

The government of the day officially estimated the deaths of 790 Muslims and 254 Hindus in a spate of communal riots across the State of Gujarat. The real number could have been a multiple of those figures – as an international human rights body estimated much later.

16 February 2002

A new snow grooming machine was introduced on the Alpine ski slopes by several ski resorts. At the implementation meeting some fears about the snow grooming machine cutting the slopes a bit too finely was dismissed by most ski resort owners as "excessive and unfounded." These machines greatly reduced expenditure on expensive ski slope curators. What was not to like for the ski resort owners?

16 May 2014

Mr. Narendra Modi won the parliamentary election with a comfortable majority and once again the promise of an egalitarian social order – "*Sabka Saath, Sabka Vikas*" paved the way for yet other bold experiment in governance.

26 May 2015

The Narendra Modi led government ensured presidential assent of a law to repatriate monies stashed away by wealthy Indians in foreign bank accounts, most notably in Switzerland.

15 July 2018

Armed with the law passed by the Modi government, the Indian investigative agencies began corralling the threads of the money trail going through Switzerland and commence strong arm tactics against Swiss banks to bring the offenders to justice to keep the "*Sabka Saath, Sabka Vikas*" slogan alive.

1 January 2019 – 21 May 2019

India goes to elections again. As with any election, the *satta bazaar* odds turn out to be far more reliable than the esteemed Lutyens Delhi psephologists. Narendra Modi returns to power with a thumping majority after decimating the combined force of the opposition. In the first week after assuming office, he renews his pledge to repatriate the stolen hoard of money in overseas bank accounts.

10 June 2022

Narendra Modi celebrates 8 years in office. In spite of significant measures by the Prime Minister himself, fringe elements in the ruling party continue to stoke the communal cauldron.

Böök I (Mid 2010)

Thë Middlë

The Melancholy of Philadelphia

The seventh-floor luxury suite of the Crowne Plaza Hotel on Chestnut Street in Philadelphia was bang in the middle of the floor. Inside, the once crisp laundered white bed sheet loosely lay over Vikas and Zainab on the king size bed. The white bed sheet covered half their bodies - the lower half.

This was not the pithy aftermath of an orgasm induced blankness and fatigue. In fact, quite to the contrary. Vikas had just disembarked from a long flight to Philadelphia and had reached his hotel and by the time he managed to shower, Zainab had arrived, and they embraced till they couldn't anymore. In the process some of the clothes had come off, but nothing much else. They lay in the bed hands tightly clasped and intertwined around Zainab's waist for several hours.

The location of the bed sheet which covered half their souls and left the other half exposed was exactly how their relationship was poised. Vikas had a job and a wife in Zurich.

Zainab had a boyfriend three doors down on Chestnut Street. None of it mattered when they embraced within the precincts of that room.

It was always the same room that Vikas asked for when he came for his prolonged business trips to Philadelphia. The business was ferrying some cash from a bank account in Switzerland to Zainab and hanging around as long as he possibly could whilst still keeping his job and wife. Just about.

They embraced for so long. The tightness of the grasp and the tenderness of the touches around the edges of the ears and the neck made it linger on till it was no longer physically possible to keep standing. Sex was not so much a call of the wild, but a perfect blending of their souls. They were in no hurry to go anywhere. On the contrary Vikas and Zainab just wanted to be still. The turmoil in their lives outside made them want this interlude really, really, badly. So, the objective was always to savour every moment, reminisce every caress, behold every embrace and be joined together in eternity. An eternity which fate had taken away from them – decisively. A decision, which neither of them could change – no matter what.

Neither willed for this to occur and neither compelled the other. There was a perfect unison of trust and harmony in their utterances. There were no second guesses, no games, no whims. One proposed and the other did unless something supernatural intervened to keep them from meeting. No questions ever asked. No grievances bottled up. They just waited. Waited for the next time. Nothing changed in this period except the intensity of their next meet.

It was like this every single time in the last three years. When it was time for Vikas to leave, he and Zainab just stood near the window, their hands criss-crossed and resting just above Zainab's navel and stood there forever. There was no hurry. No fervent stolen kisses. Nothing wildly exciting. In fact, it was the dulling down of excitement which they loved in their moments together. They could sit long and just criss-cross their fingers, with Vikas sometimes kissing Zainab's knuckles. He loved to take his index finger to move her curls behind her ears as they sat, eyes locked together and muttered how deep their love was for each other.

There was obviously a lot to talk about given the state of their relationships – with each other and certain other third parties intricately involved with their lives. Both desperately wanted to be with each other, but their circumstances were beyond them. So, they did not really foretell the future but tried to savour the present. They were grateful for each other's company and needed each other to stay in their lives. Vikas and Zainab were like the mysterious elixir for each other and could only shudder at what life may have been for them but for their chance meeting.

As Zainab shifted and moved her head to rest on Vikas's chest, she could hear the thud of his heartbeat. She still remembered the first time she had been that close to him. Clearly his heart rate had improved since then. At least that's what she consoled herself with all the other times when Vikas was in Zurich. Vikas loved kissing her neck and gently nibbling her ear lobes when she was resting in that position. They could whisper loads of things to each other during those moments. Many times, entire days passed with them being in bed – not in some passionate tantric sex postures- but pretty much connected through their souls – sitting or lying in close proximity. The mere touch of each other reinvigorated their souls from the past and current baggage. There was clearly no shortage in the baggage department. It's not that they unloaded onto each other indiscriminately. It was more the process of being together that they were sometimes able to untangle vexed nerves of their immediate and more distant past. Trying to re-discover a bit of their former selves. Their same former selves which never got a chance to meet and unite. Instead, they met when a whole lot of baggage had accumulated. Although secretly they felt cheated at their chance together at life having been denied, but yet there was gratitude at having met albeit in challenging circumstances.

But three years had gone by. How long could this go on? Neither broached the topic, because neither had any inkling of the solution. Far from the solution, neither even had the energy to commence yet another battle to move anything forward.

Clearly both had been through the dungeons of their emotions and found light in each other. Maybe it would be like this forever. Maybe it would not be. Neither knew. Also, life had made them question their past assumptions. But what was wonderful about them being together was the complete faith in each other that things would be alright. At least so far. There were sometimes far away niggling doubts that things couldn't be so perfect but the past three years had not displayed any of that.

The trouble with any middle point in a relationship, is the certainty of the past journey and the uncertainty of the future path. Equally, the past journey in the case of Vikas and Zainab, did not really pave their future path with roses. Actually, exactly the opposite. There were painful episodes to close out, relationships to rectify, lies to be opened up, truths to be faced. All in all, a saga of unpleasantness which threatened to incinerate the little nest that Vikas and Zainab had built. But how long could one stay in this nest?

Böök II

Thë Bëginning (1968–1992)

Magnus – The Badshah of Zurich

When Magnus Montgomery entered the elite world of Swiss private banking, having regional expertise was encouraged by banks in Switzerland. What that really meant was for bankers to target acquiring clients from a particular country and convince those clients to park their monies in banks in Switzerland.

Given Magnus studied Asian History for his undergraduate degree at the University of St Gallan, he obviously had very little attention for the sciences and technology. What intrigued him were some of the Asian nations whose history he had fleetingly studied while trying to get a university degree. So, when he was asked by the Banque Merck Privee to fill out his preferred market in his graduate application form, he had without thinking ticked "South - East Asia." Not to be different from his cohort who mainly filled out USA or other European countries like Italy, Germany, France and the like, but purely because something told him this could be interesting. He of course never knew that this one tick would change Swiss private banking's destiny altogether.

Magnus had so often read that those who dare will be fuelled on by lady luck. Or at any rate not be let down or tormented. So, when he was assigned as a graduate trainee in the much - ridiculed new South - East Asia team, for the first few years, it felt like trying to play catch up forever on his friends working in the more mature and developed teams of the bank.

Till such time as Mrs. Indira Gandhi in faraway India in 1970 started murmuring to her inner circle about the political plaudits to be had by abolishing the privy purse – in other words a king's ransom paid by the Union of India to the erstwhile royalty in return for them having hurriedly acceded to the Union of India on the eve of Indian Independence.

For those like Magnus unaware of the complex glue that held together the Union of India post the Declaration of Independence, the privy purse was one such mechanism. Crude in its application and sure shot in its outcome. Till such time at least till any other outcome was not an option for the recipients. Or when Mrs. Gandhi thought that abolishing the privy purse which impacted circa 550 rulers of erstwhile princely states would bring her disproportionate electoral gain from the vassals and subjects of those 550 plus rulers – a humungous vote bank that could not be ignored.

What Mrs. Gandhi had not accounted for was the windfall gain and the career moving impact that this decision had on Magnus. When the first prince arrived from faraway Junagadh with a suitcase full of US Dollars. Then another. Then yet another. And the flow didn't ebb. Not for a very long time.

Magnus could not quite comprehend why and how they were landing up at his offices and why suddenly the underperforming and poorly staffed South - East Asia team was back in the game. Actually, not just action, some serious groovy moves. Since none of the senior bankers in the vicinity knew or bothered to keep track of these developments, Magnus was quietly ratcheting up his cash deposits from these Indian princes going rogue. Actually, not rogue. Just declaring independence of the financial kind from the Union of India. They had liquidated assets for a long time knowing fully well, this Sword of Damocles would fall upon them when they started becoming political pygmies. And when that occurred most were not taken by surprise. The only one being taken by any sort of surprise was Magnus.

He had trouble counting the monies, since they were coming in an avalanche. Magnus' rise was akin to the proverbial underdog in a world cup league game. No one knew him, no one expected anything of him and when it happened, people only could gasp.

First, all the suitcases of cash that he had collected, which in Swiss banking parlance was called assets under management, surpassed the entire Luxembourg team, then East Europe, then Russia and when it toppled Belgium, the senior management of BMP woke up to see what the hell was happening. How an Associate Banker - a one man army was now managing more assets and generating more revenue from those assets than other established teams with huge overheads and headcounts. And that was a disastrous move.

As with any management move, instead of providing impetus, they slowed down Magnus' ability to organise this trade and started being curious about how they could institutionalise the business. That irked Magnus given there had been no objective to institutionalise him all these years when the South - East team was just a diversity box ticker within BMP. And that was it.

Magnus left the building. And with him left a rainbow parade of a motley crowd of Indian rulers and princes and their prized assets. The biggest *faux pas* in the history of BMP and a masterstroke of Banque Wedderburn Privee. That started the magnificent rise of Banque Wedderburn

Privee on the Swiss banking horizon and the undisputed standing of Magnus Montgomery as the *badshah* of South - East Asian private banking.

Except he never quite understood how geographically, India fitted into the description of South - East Asia. Not that he understood many things that BMP did and had a deep dislike of management of any kind. The founding family of Banque Wedderburn Privee understood that well and had left explicit instructions with the management to not bother Magnus and give him a free hand. For ten years, Magnus' assets grew by an astronomical 45-60 per cent year on year. And then it stopped.

These rulers had by then muled all their wealth across to Switzerland and they had no productive ventures to generate any cash flow. Some of the more enterprising varieties were now contemplating joint ventures with some hospitality groups in India to transform their decrepit palaces into luxury resorts to generate some spare change.

Magnus by now had a fantastic network across the Indian subcontinent thanks to hanging out at the debauched parties of the Maharaja of Jodhpur and the Rajmata of Gwalior. Their parties could put to shame even the vilest of orgies of the Ottoman Empire. But that was purely business for Magnus. The asset rich and cash poor *hoi oligoi,* could not resist rubbing shoulders with the new industry captains of the oncoming industrial revolution in India. These were a pack of hungry wolves who went after whatever resources nature or government had to offer and monetised it quickly by selling to international buyers. The trouble with such transactions was that the government tried to take away too much of the share from these wolves.

Thereby started Magnus' second growth curve ensuring safe custody of part of the sale consideration in Swiss accounts – far away from the prying eyes of the Indian government and completely legal. Thereafter for the next round of accessing government resources these monies left one account within Banque Wedderburn Privee and entered another account. All under the management of Magnus. His assets never depleted. Only grew.

The legend of Magnus grew by leaps and bounds. Just when people had started saying that Magnus' growth had stalled, he had jumped onto the next big gravy train. This gravy train had no destination and no stops. Till such time as the government couldn't offer up its natural resources for a song. And that time was very far away.

Magnus controlled the entire value chain of this entirely legitimate and overboard transactional network. Swiss laws encouraged this trade and Indian laws did not forbid it – what was there not to like. And therein lay the secret sauce of his success – no interlopers, no management, no oversight and no time wasters. Magnus valued his time intensely. Whether on client meetings or on holiday - speed was his drug. And that drug was consumed copiously on the Alpine slopes on skis. Speed on the slopes opened his mind and aligned his neurons to new ways of business with this crowd of politicos and embezzlers. He treated them with due care and diligence, but nothing personal. His interest was purely professional.

Böök III

Bëförë thë Bëginning (1975–1992)

Back to the Olden Times - Virbhadra – Love's Tempest in Betrayal's Hamlet

1. Somewhere in Virbhadra Town in Present Day Uttarakhand

Varun Dixit clambered up the last flight of spiral stairs opening up to the vast area atop Water Tank No. 5 of the Virbhadra township. The water tank or *tanki* as it was called in their township used to be totally white on the outside at the time it was built. The interior which served as a convenient meeting or rather mating spot for couples and other renegades of Virbhadra society had never received a coat of paint since inception. It carried the coarseness of the cement mix dutifully blazened and baked with pigeon droppings in the tropical sun which were subsequently rain drenched and sun-dried.

There the familiar, comforting, and lovely waist length *henna* enriched locks of Zainab Siddiqui, tilting gently against the winds caught his eye. His breathing relaxed. His now practised eyes did a quick scan to make sure they were the only ones there. The mofussil expanse that one could see from that vantage point was strangely serene. Too far up to actually partake in the din of the million conversations underway beneath. But the vista of the uneven concrete developments, equally weather worn, some with clothes of an equally discoloured variety adorning their frontage was strangely romantic from that height. The clothes signified a lot about the workforce - factory workers or office sitters. The distinction was the office worker trousers were wider at the waist while the worker shirts were worn out at the sleeves.

Zainab had made it clear this would be the last time she would see him. Till such time as the epic Class 12 Board Examinations did not conclude. But she had said so last time as well. That was a week ago, when he was literally left dangling from her third-floor flat balcony to avoid detection by Zainab's mother.

This occurred when Zainab's mother, Mrs. Filzah Siddiqui returned early from her invigilation duty at the IDPL Inter College. One of the avowed objectives of the Uttar Pradesh Board of High School and Intermediate Education was that teachers were sent to far flung places for invigilation during the board examinations across the state to minimise cases of cheating. These places were usually a good four to five hours away from their normal place of duty. However, only in the case of Mrs. Filzah Siddiqui was she assigned

IDPL Inter College which at her usual languid pace of walking consumed no more than twenty-five minutes.

Varun had feigned mock rage about Mr. Rana Siddiqui, Zainab's father somehow pulling rank with the IDPL Inter College which was within Virbhadra township to ensure her mother did not have far to travel for her invigilation duties during the board examinations.

Not that Varun's heart bled for the cause of board examination fairness. Given Zainab and he only got all of half an hour maximum to spend in private after their tuitions and before Mrs. Siddiqui arrived on the scene, he was most upset at the unfairness of the duty allocation. Zainab had brushed off suggestions of her father being that influential as to manage her mother's exam duty roster, while he had fiddled with her exquisite waist length curls, head on her lap.

Mrs. Siddiqui's exam roster ensured Varun and Zainab never got beyond first base of kissing, holding hands and clumsy hugging within the confines of the drawing room in her father's Type-III government flat within IDPL Colony. The four storey structures housed four flats on each floor. Therefore, getting into Zainab's flat without setting off wagging tongues ensured all manner of guile and deception unknown even to international spies.

When Varun had to foist himself on the external precipice of Zainab's flat to make sure Mrs. Filzah Siddiqui did not see him while keeping her shoes in the balcony, the fable of the *Daksha Yagna* that his grandmother used to tell him as a child ran through his mind.

Suddenly at that very moment the fable became crystal clear in all details. It had taken place in Virbhadra several aeons ago - perhaps on the same spot where he was swinging between certain death by falling or certain humiliation by detection by Mrs. Siddiqui. So, while Varun Dixit hung between the twin rocks of death and humiliation, the fable became all too clear in his mind.

The same *Daksha Yagna* or a magnificent religious ritual, which *Lord Shiva* had wrecked by invoking *Virbhadra*, a particularly malevolent mutant of himself. All because, King Daksha who was Lord Brahma's son had not invited Shiva's wife, Sati for the grand *yagna*. While he felt the black algal soot embedded in the erstwhile orange cream walls of the Type-III building starting to wipe clean threatening to maim if not kill him altogether, he remembered the next part.

King Dakhsa had disliked Lord Shiva because in spite of him having forbidden Sati, his daughter, she went on to marry Lord Shiva. But who could withstand the charm of Lord Shiva? Sati was no different. So, when despite express instructions from Lord Shiva to save certain humiliation at hands of King Daksha, Sati went to King Daksha's *yagna* and was insulted sufficiently enough to immolate herself,

Lord Shiva invoked *Virbhadra* and destroyed the *yagna* and decapitated King Daksha.

Varun at that point did not know whether to feel bad for Lord Shiva at the loss of his wife in such tragic circumstances or King Daksha at the loss of his daughter, Sati or for the departed soul Sati herself. Because Varun himself was on the verge of coming close to becoming a departed soul or at any rate an amputated one. The only saving grace, unlike the *Daksha Yajna,* was that this battle was being played out without any public scrutiny. At least none that Varun could see.

Mrs. Siddiqui after leaving her shoes in the balcony had quickly retreated to the inner chambers for her evening prayers, leaving enough time for Varun to clamber back up and scoot from the main entrance. Never again he had promised himself. Then a voice told him- who was he kidding? How could someone withstand the allure of Zainab? How could he not take further risks to his life and limb to be with Zainab?

2.

One of the advantages of life on the sprawling IDPL Colony was the communal anonymity that it offered. Even though everyone or at any rate one family member worked for the same company - the all-mighty white elephant - the Indian Drug and Pharmaceutical Limited, there was little or no social interaction between the various segments of the colony.

The socialisation was mainly either within departmental colleagues or equals or building mates, which anyway ensured departmental parity. So, even though Varun Dixit's trudge from his father's allotted Type-V quarter to Zainab's was no more than half an hour, the social isolation between those two bands of IDPL officers had not been bridged since its inception in 1967. And it would never be bridged.

These things were not apparent when Varun and Zainab met in class 11 at the IDPL Kendriya Vidyalaya, when Zainab's father had been transferred from Hyderabad to Virbhadra.

Varun had spent his entire life in the IDPL Colony in Virbhadra and was familiar with every nook and cranny and took great delight in showing Zainab some of the things off the beaten track. Zainab had left behind a massive city and her entire lifetime of friends and family in Hyderabad. Therefore, to find a friend in Varun so quickly was solace. It not only made the transition easier; it brought about a spring in her step every morning while getting ready for school.

Varun's rimless bespectacled deep brown eyes held such a degree of sincerity on his oval shaped brown face that she had after some time abandoned some of the religious proscriptions that her mother used to remind her of periodically since attaining puberty. Too few, Varun used to rue.

"I never thought I would see you again," exclaimed Varun.

Zainab's smile spread all over her dimples on both cheeks exposing her high canines on both sides. She had just gotten over a bad case of teenage acne and had much more confidence in her smile now. She flicked one of her curls away from her face and hugged Varun and gently pecked him on his right cheek and said, "it was a close shave, indeed."

"Close shave? More like a death sentence."

Both Varun and Zainab laughed in unison, neither wanting to let go of the other. Neither knew what the future held. Neither cared. The excitement of the moment. The gentle wind throwing Zainab's curls onto Varun's face atop Water Tank No. 5 in Virbhadra township was a moment that both wanted to last forever.

Varun held Zainab's face in his hands and just looked into her gorgeous light hazel eyes and kissed her lips. That's when the factory siren sounded its first hooting alarm. This meant that the machines would shut in another fifteen minutes and the workers would start trooping back to their respective quarters.

That sadly also meant that Water Tank No.5 would be inspected for one last time top to bottom. It was time to go. Varun clasped Zainab tight and kissed her moist lips for what felt like a lifetime. Zainab disengaged and left climbing down the one hundred and eighty odd stairs carefully. Her eyes alert to any moving objects. All clear. Varun left precisely five minutes later. It was a practised drill for two years. No trouble so far.

3.

Trouble meanwhile was brewing in the Siddiqui family. Mrs. Filzah Siddiqui's sister's husband's elder stepbrother's son was getting married. And getting married the next week. Even though Mrs. Siddiqui had been nagging Rana Saheb as he liked to be called at home about going there for a few weeks now, little by way of a plan had been made.

"Zainab's board exams would be over by then," ventured Mrs. Siddiqui.

"I know, but you know it is difficult to get leave sanctioned at such short notice," responded Rana Saheb.

"Short notice? I had told you about this at least two months ago."

"There is a lot of work pressure right now."

"Work pressure? There are at least five thousand people who work in this branch of IDPL. If you take off for two days, will the operations stop?"

"You will not understand, Filzah."

"Alright. Make me understand. You are the Senior Purchase Officer of IDPL in Virbhadra. What could be so important on two days that your absence will bring this company to a standstill? There are at least seven others in our building itself, who work in the Purchase Department. None of them can officiate on your behalf for two days?"

"I will try tomorrow," resigned Rana Saheb.

"Also, it is only Amroha we are going to. All of one hundred and sixty kilometres. If it is such a pressing issue, we can come back right after the *Nikkah*. *Khali peth*." The *khali peth* bit was the sting in the tail.

"Let's talk tomorrow. Also, this is not like your school job that I can call in sick *jab man hua*."

The last sentence rolled off Rana Saheb's tongue almost involuntarily. He did not mean to cause hurt. But given he had to literally go around the IDPL top brass officialdom to ensure his wife got a job at the IDPL Inter College as a

Chemistry teacher, made him entitled to use it in self - defence. Not really. When his eyes met Filzah's, they both knew it was below the belt and ought not be used lightly. After all, hadn't she sacrificed so much for this posting?

Mrs. Filzah Siddiqui grimaced but did not push the matter further. It was not so much the lure of attending a wedding or even the social strictures that came with missing a family obligation that bothered her. Actually, she just wanted to go somewhere away from Virbhadra. Even if it was Amroha. Though her elder sister, Parveen had married and lived there for over twenty years, she had never had the occasion to visit. Parveen would come down to Hyderabad for all the vacations with her family.

The only thing she knew about Amroha was that it was famous for enormous mango orchards and the *rohu* fish that inhabited the Sot River in abundance. The Sot River which somehow delineated the town across class structures. Not very neatly, but still provided some sort of a handle to understand the class hierarchies.

Even then at least, it would be a much larger version of the IDPL colony. Mrs. Siddiqui had found the hierarchy within the IDPL colony claustrophobic. It seemed odd to her that Type-III residents could not freely socialise with Type-IV residents. Even the fact that her husband was entitled to a Type-IV flat, but on account of his sudden transfer from

Hyderabad had to settle for a Type-III flat made no difference.

She did not know if similar conditions prevailed in the IDPL colony in Hyderabad, because she never had to live there. So, when Rana Saheb was asked to transfer to Virbhadra on account of some new foreign collaboration programme, she was apprehensive. Her apprehensions turned to reality, when she figured that she had not been transported into a microcosm of Hyderabad. Rather a totally different beast with totally different jungle rules of social bonding. Her Type-III residents block was all that her social circle could comprise of. Not by choice, rather by the class consensus that passed off as social niceties.

Her status as a secondary school level Chemistry teacher warded off many other homemakers in her flat complex. Her religious identity had never felt as stark as it did in Virbhadra. In Hyderabad, it never mattered. Here, being a working woman coupled with her religious identity made her isolation absolute and complete.

Rana Saheb had sensed this could be an issue early on and had made gargantuan efforts to ensure she got employed at the IDPL Inter College. So, even the thought of a two -day sojourn to Amroha seemed like a spiritual spa for Mrs. Siddiqui.

The walls of her house here gnawed her innards. There was not an ounce of homely familiarity that she could bring in spite of her best efforts. These purpose - built flats in 1970 had long outlived their shelf life, but a sick government undertaking that IDPL in reality was, could ill afford to upgrade them. Even after badgering Rana Saheb for arranging extra funds and labour to rectify some aspects, the flat in the last two years whilst civil was far away from being called a home by a stretched imagination. The exteriors of the flats had possibly been sparkling white when the dinosaurs roamed the earth. That too, possibly – nothing in their current form betrayed any hope of these flats ever having been pristine in any way. Now they were an ashen mix of algal green and fungal black. Very similar to the overall financial health and viability of IDPL as an enterprise.

The tropical climes at the foothills of the Himalayas meant everything from buildings to clothes descended to a dull median colour very soon after being exposed to the elements. The staircase to her third floor flat resembled Dracula's teeth knocked out a million times over by Muhammad Ali's blows. Thanks, in large measure to the Bharat Gas cylinders which had to be taken up and down the stairs every month.

In spite of the turmoil within and the fact that Rana Saheb had for the last two years been largely detached from the running of the household, she always put up a brave face in front of Zainab. Rana Saheb wasn't always so detached – she just could not figure out yet what had changed in Virbhadra. She fervently hoped Zainab would grow up and out of Virbhadra. What scared Mrs. Siddiqui most was that many of the children in the age bracket that Zainab belonged to seemed to be content running micro-enterprises from within the government accommodation.

One floor down, Mrs. Pokhriyal's twenty - year - old son was content repairing electrical goods for Virbhadra residents. Another floor down, she had overheard, Mrs. Uniyal's daughter who looked all of seventeen did a pretty good pedicure for Type-III ladies.

Mrs. Siddiqui's own educational credentials coupled with schooling Zainab at a reasonably good Hyderabad private school till class 10 did not allow for her to even start to contemplate such forms of self-employment for Zainab.

It did not bother Mrs. Siddiqui in the least that the whole of Virbhadra had not a single mosque. Neither did it bother her that many of her neighbours carried out noisy marches to the Neeb Karoli Baba Ashram or the Hanuman Mandir located within the precincts of the IDPL colony. She was also not offended when Mrs. Pokhriyal oblivious to her religious identity invited her to join a bare foot procession to the Neelkanth Mahadev Temple with her and others from the Type-III quarters. She would not have minded going along for the jolly, except she could not take off five days from the IDPL Inter College where she was fast gaining a reputation as a safe pair of hands with Chemistry – with the students and other teachers alike.

However, she now retrospectively thanked her stars that she had politely excused herself, because that procession was knowingly or unknowingly directed through an area of lower caste settlements in Rishikesh, and which had for some unknown reason resulted in an outbreak of violence. Unknown to Mrs. Pokhriyal because she was as five - star *bhakt*. And when one is a *bhakt*, one becomes blind to the politics and commerce which feeds off such *bhakti*.

So, every year, such violence was instigated and some *bhakts* on either side were lucky to escape with minor or negligible bruises. Equally, every year some unlucky ones perished either coming in way of a stray stone not intended to kill. Or like on one occasion when an irate Station House Officer ordered the local police to resort to firing bullets to disperse the crowd. Except he did not specify the direction of the bullets. Needless to mention the frontline of the lower caste colony perished. But the goodness of the *bhakts* is that such incidents howsoever engineered are taken as retribution of the gods for past evil deeds and absorbed within their otherwise overflowing ocean of sadness and misery.

The buccaneers of such processions were busy counting contributions and votes for the next election. Roughly every injury rightly channelised brought in about 40 assured votes and every death about 100. Simple matrix. No emotions there. Such mobilisations were after all essential to keep one's voting army war ready – who knows which election is called when. And as was said once famously and equally stupidly: the path to Delhi passes through Uttar Pradesh referring to the apparent heft of the 80 Lok Sabha Members of Parliament that the state contributed. Clearly, this pathway had to be kept well lubricated and a few deaths, amputations, limb impairments or other misery here and there were just collateral damage for a larger national goal – service of the poor. Wasn't that after all the goal of all politics in this country and this was after all the State of Uttar Pradesh – the holy grail of Indian politics had to be woven from these very strands.

Mrs. Siddiqui considered her religion to be a wholly private matter, one to regulate her own and her immediate family's ethical moorings and values, but not one for public demonstration. Again, when she spoke to Zainab, she wanted her to have no less opportunities on account of her religion. But she did sorely feel that Zainab lacked friends in this new setup and there was nothing she could possibly do to replace them except spend more and more time with her. She was obviously in the dark room as far as Varun's friendly overtures towards Zainab had been concerned. Not by accident, but by great guile and deception employed by the two.

4.

The structure of the IDPL Colony was very supportive of the *varna* system. Unless someone went out of their way for anthropological curiosity reasons, they would never have to go lower down the pecking order. The General Manager's bungalow was within easy access to one of the main gates to the expansive estate and within easy walking distance to the corporate office complex. That ensured he never had to go any further into the depths of the IDPL Colony unless he wished to. And what was really there to wish for in the dilapidated state of the remaining estate!

Then the weather - beaten Type–V bungalows stood in eerie isolation from the Type-IV five storey flat complexes separated by at least the length of five football fields. That ensured that Type-IV officers walking back from the factory premises would keep a keen eye out for any early returners among the Type-V officers and mark their evening greetings.

The Type-III, Type-II and Type I quarters diminished proportionately in square footage of living space and increased in the distance from the factory premises. Thus, ironically, many of the ones who had to report earliest for the call of duty at the IDPL factories lived the furthest. And as if that were not enough to distinguish the various grades of IDPL employees, the estate maintenance department ensured that the upkeep of the different quarters was in direct proportion to the seniority of the occupants. Which essentially meant that funds and materials did not penetrate the IDPL colony to its fullest depth.

Whilst the General Manager's bungalow would receive a fresh coat of paint every year, Type-I apartments were lucky to have an overflowing sewage tank repaired only when the stink threatened to overrun the *varna* system and permeate up the hierarchy. Besides that, the lower down the hierarchy one went, any sign of IDPL's estate maintenance became less commonplace. This had led to a mushrooming local economy of plumbers, fitters, drillers and the like operating from the demarcated shopping complexes within the IDPL colony.

The beauty of this *varna* system were the invisible lines and undeclared segregation among the various parts of the colony. Perfect social harmony. One could only transcend it by going up the seniority ladder within IDPL. But there too the recruitment and promotion rules came to the aid of maintaining this social façade. A Type-I officer could not retire as the General Manager, even if he spent three hundred years in service with exemplary merit. Very unlike General Motors. But then IDPL was no General Motors. Far from it. It was dedicated to the service of the nation and so that was the sole goal it pursued at huge expense to the taxpayer without much by way of return. Actually zilch.

Varun Dixit was thus born within this system in a Type-IV flat, where his father moved from Haldwani holding a master's degree in pharmacology from the G.B Pant Institute in Pantnagar. So, Varun's life was somehow caged within this tripod of Pantnagar, his *nanihal*, Haldwani, his *dadihal* and Virbhadra, his *karmabhoomi*. And so far in his *karmabhoomi* he had succeeded in breaking down every hierarchy in having the girl of his dreams by his side. The colony hierarchy – the biggest caste system of all, the religious fault line and also the regional divide. So, when a Type V scion hailing from a Brahmin family of western Uttar Pradesh falls for a Type III Muslim girl from Hyderabad, all sorts of matrices become jammed. Except in this case nothing got jammed. Instead, what happened, Varun could never have imagined in his wildest dreams and Zainab in her recurring nightmares.

5.

The town of Amroha resided almost in a parallel universe to that of Virbhadra. All said and done, IDPL had contributed substantially to the education gathering credo of the colony. The *varna* system aside, every category of worker or officer at IDPL was assured of a subsidised education for their offspring.

Meanwhile, the talk of the town in Amroha appeared to be a spanking new compound coming up under the aegis of the *Madrasa Islamiya Arbiya Afakul Uloom*. The contractors, mostly *baniyas* had no qualms queueing up and throwing lavish lunches for the management board members of the Islamic seminary to get a toehold on the plethora of building work contracts.

Equally, the *baniya* contractors, who assiduously steered clear of meat in their homes, ensured that the best *kebabchi* in town made the meat delicacies at these feasts. Nothing wrong, except their choice was very clear. Commerce first, religion second. Though not many were lucky enough in Amroha town to make such explicit and clear choices and live by them.

Mrs. Siddiqui's sister, Parveen was married into the family which was managing the *Madrasa Islamiya* since its foundation in 1932. There were lawsuits in local courts pending since the same period challenging the ability of one family to control what was in effect a public charitable trust. Parveen's husband Mian Ashfaqullah had astutely managed a complicit bureaucracy and local courts alike. To the point where even the legal recollection of the character of the institution was obfuscated in government records beyond repair. Which in the parlance of Uttar Pradesh translated into perfect title of the land and assets. In other words, perfection of the absolute and total entitlement to the land in favour of the usurper or possessor with little left by way of legal redress in favour of the challenger.

Neatly carved out from the seminary compound was a sprawling bungalow occupied by Mian Ashfaqullah's family. Outside the wrought iron gate were gold embossed letters declaring him as the President. No suffix. No prefix. But the average or below average onlooker were left in no doubt about the grandeur of Mian Saheb's presidency and what all was subject or forcefully subjugated to his suzerainty.

For most of the petty visitors to the seminary who contributed earnings in coins and soiled notes from heavy toil either in illegal mines or foundries, Mian Saheb would never descend from his high horse. They were of course the fodder which allowed him to feed his property acquisition engine. After all, it was for their benefit that he was running this scheme, wasn't it.

It was the most pious deed and of course *Allah* would look after them directly. He had bigger things to look after. Like the donations from non - resident Muslims in the form of *zakat*. After all, social heft in a small town like Amroha was in direct proportion to the amount of tangible and intangible assets one controlled. It mattered little that Mian Saheb was not the beneficiary of such assets, rather only the custodian. In fact, the destitute, the disabled and the depressed Muslim folk who came to the seminary in the hope of succour, left pretty much the same way they had come. They of course accepted such treatment as the will of *Allah*. The will of *Allah* as translated by Mian Saheb in his flowing sparkling white *shervani*, peaked black all weather skull cap with his beady eyes behind his gold rimmed glasses. His salt and pepper beard hid a childhood outbreak of small - pox in Amroha. Many similarly aged as Mian Saheb at that time did not live to hide the scars behind a beard. They died young.

That brush with death, where timely intervention at one of the better hospitals in Delhi saved Mian Saheb taught him one lesson. Maintain distance from the unwashed masses, who frequented the seminary. They were the source and sustenance of such diseases and the further he stayed away from them the better he would be. Since then, he had no other life - threatening illnesses of course and since taking over as the custodian of the seminary affairs, the financial health of it had never been better.

Because Mian Saheb unlike his father ran it like an enterprise. An enterprise where the margin between input and output must be significantly large to make it worthwhile. And once it was worthwhile, the number of claimants on the output ought to be very tiny. With these two principles, the business of the *Madrasa Islamiya* flourished and so did Mian Saheb's heft in Amroha society.

Rana Saheb had a one - sided dislike towards Mian Saheb's way of life. Mian Saheb, given his view of himself and of the world at large from his seventh floor centrally air - conditioned offices in one of the Mecca facing spires of the seminary was totally oblivious of Rana Saheb's feelings towards him. On the contrary, when he had learnt about Rana Saheb's transfer to Virbhadra, the first thing he had done was to scope out a parcel of neglected land within the IDPL colony. The perfect candidate to usurp under the guise of a manufactured *waqf*.

Given his long years in running the seminary and having seen his father in action before being handed the mantle, he had ceased to distinguish between what was service to self and what was service to *Allah*. In any event, the pupils of the seminary and the town at large gave him enough reason to smear the already fine line between self and *Allah*. Not that the absence of such adulation would have anyway deterred Mian Saheb's resolve, but it helped cloak his ventures with a veneer of public service.

6.

Meanwhile, a mere 31 Kilometres Away in Moradabad, the *ghunghat* which was first thrust upon Rishika Pradhan her on her nineteenth birthday. The ever - watchful eye of her mother Mrs. Uma Pradhan had caught many a roving eye resting for longer than normal on Rishika in *Peetal Mandi*.

Mrs. Uma Pradhan had spent the better part of the last two years escorting Rishika back from a corner of *Peetal Mandi*. The corner where the rickety Kedarnath Girdharilal Khatri College bus dropped and picked up Rishika.

Her husband and Rishika's father, Rakesh Pradhan who had a brassware shop on the opposite end of *Peetal Mandi* never had the time to drop or pick up Rishika. So busy he was with his travel between Moradabad and Delhi and at times to Mumbai. Rakesh Pradhan only travelled by Uttar Pradesh State Transport Corporation buses to Delhi.

The ostensible reason for Rakesh Pradhan's frequent travel was to lug large crates of brass idols and candle ware to customs houses in Delhi and Mumbai. His business model was simple. He had over the years built some contacts in Delhi who placed specific orders for a certain number of items and paid cash in advance. Then Rakesh Pradhan had to collect the desired number and grade of brass items from *Peetal Mandi* and have them packed into boxes of certain specifications. To avoid paying commercial rates of transportation Rakesh Pradhan had them loaded onto the UPSRTC buses and lugged them to Delhi. His contacts would invariably be waiting with a minivan near the ISBT Terminus in Sarai Kale Khan in Delhi. Rakesh Pradhan's work ended at that point, and he would invariably take the next bus back to Moradabad.

Never once had he succumbed to the allure of Delhi beyond the collection and delivery of those boxes at the inter-state bus terminal at Sarai Kale Khan. But doing this journey sometimes almost three to four times a week left precious little time for him to attend to the fatherly duties in relation to Rishika. On many a rickety ride back to Moradabad, while resting his wide fair forehead against the blackened iron window grill of the UPSRTC bus, he had wondered for how much longer he could keep doing this.

How much longer could he continue to procure large brass candle stands with hollowed interiors for two hundred rupees apiece and sell them for one thousand rupees apiece to his Delhi contacts. Having done this for a good twenty - five years when the margin was even higher, all his Delhi contacts, save one, were telling him the market all around was collapsing. Rakesh Pradhan never quite understood who would want those ugly unwieldy candle stands. But he never asked questions. He did as he was told. This one exception to the dwindling margin game was Vikas. Vikas Kumar. The man who changed his life in more ways than he could have ever imagined.

Rakesh Pradhan was an outlier among the business community in *Peetal Mandi*. His genteel nature and soft features made him stand out from the other battle hardened and unequally weary copper traders in Moradabad. It was also this quality that had enabled him to spread his business directly to some exporters in Delhi, enabling him to earn a higher margin. Since he had avoided the middlemen and was seen as lugging boxes to Delhi in UPSRTC buses, he never was taken as a serious player in that community. Being under the radar suited him just fine.

7.

When Vikas Kumar had first set himself up running a small travel agency in West Punjabi Bagh, he turned over little more than two lakh rupees every year. His customers were mainly some shop owners in the automobile trade who travelled a few times to Coimbatore a year and an annual vacation in Mussorie or Shimla or thereabouts.

Vikas would have continued to earn that amount for the rest of his life, but for having the chance meeting with Magnus Montgomery. Magnus was a Swiss national who was looking for the nearest police station in West Punjabi Bagh having had his briefcase stolen which contained his passport. What Magnus never told Vikas was that the passport was the least important of the items stolen.

When the police recovered Magnus' briefcase from a petty part time thief in Mansarovar Gardens, they had found everything intact and were puzzled by torn pieces of Indian currency. The area inspector not wanting to add to his burgeoning caseload of far more heinous crimes closed the case. However, by this time Magnus' tourist visa on his Swiss passport had expired. Whilst, the police sympathised with Magnus' plight, they drove him to Vikas' ramshackle shop and asked him to sort out this mess and let the police concentrate on keeping the Republic of West Punjabi Bagh safe.

Magnus had been impressed by Vikas' prompt service and his agility with moving paper between government departments. So, when Magnus got his stay regularised, he was more than happy with paying a token service fee of one lakh rupees. Vikas in his shrewd yet simplistic mind was hoping to have made five thousand after having quoted eight thousand rupees! Though that was peanuts for the job that Magnus got done so efficiently and without breaking sweat, it was roughly half of what Vikas earned in one year. Magnus had promised to return and had asked Vikas to keep in touch.

From the documents he had submitted for Magnus's visa renewal, he had figured out that Magnus worked as a Managing Director at Banque Wedderburn Privee in Zurich. That somehow lit up fantastic sights of Kajol in a red minidress. Drunk on cognac, prancing the boulevards of Interlaken on a horse drawn carriage from *Dilwale Dulhania Le Jayenge*. While waiting for the faxed documents to arrive at Sharma Photostat in Janakpuri, Magnus had told Vikas that he worked for a bank in Switzerland.

The first reaction of Vikas on seeing the letterhead of Banque Wedderburn Privee coming out of a soot black oil-stained fax machine at Sharma Photostat was surprise. Surprise that English spellings were possibly not the strongest suite at the bank Magnus' worked for. After all, even him with his bachelor's degree in commerce from Dayal Singh College he could spell "bank" the right way. Why him, even the *chotu* at Sharma Photostat could have spelt bank the right way. Actually, anyone in West Punjabi Bagh would have aced the competition to spell "bank" in English. That's how the local economy was – everyone knew four letter words really well – whether in English or Hindi.

He did share his concern with Magnus, anxious that the visa renewal officers in the Ministry of External Affairs in Delhi may raise an alarm. Magnus had assured him that the spelling was indeed correct. Not one to look a gift horse in the mouth, Vikas had submitted the papers as obtained together with a hefty mark-up on the application fees. Magnus never complained. Magnus never cared. That was the nature of Magnus. Forget the pennies and the pounds will come rolling in.

Magnus never wasted any effort on saving expenses. He was always the big picture sort of guy. Just the sort of guy Vikas wanted to be, but his expertise was always called upon for tidying up petty documentation. Well, whatever paid the bills, thought Vikas. The whole episode and his interaction with Magnus had left Vikas a bit confused. None of Magnus' bits added up- but in the typical aloof West Punjabi Bagh way of "*sannu key*" he let it be.

8.

Magnus did return after six months. But in the meanwhile, Vikas had upgraded himself from his Bajaj brand scooter to a fourth hand Maruti 1000. It was largely thanks to Inspector Khullar's generosity in driving hapless foreigners with lost passports and expired visas to him. Inspector Khullar did it purely from a hassle prevention perspective and not a rent seeking one.

In any case Vikas' shop and his *halaat* would not make for rich pickings. *Jitne ka ghagra phatega utne ka maza nahin aayega* was Inspector Khullar's constant refrain. Vikas did not mind it one bit and lapped up the business walking through the door driven in *lal batti* vehicles.

When Vikas drove up the sharp incline of the driveway at the Taj Palace Hotel on Sardar Patel Marg, his greenish brown

Maruti 1000 sputtered for breath and nearly gave up. Vikas pressed down his three - year - old Agra-made fake Red Tape shoe hard on the accelerator and in the bust up between worn out car and worn - out shoe, Vikas made it up. Only just.

The dour curled moustached doorman looked at Vikas up and down and could not figure out whether or not to complete his crisp salute. In the end the doorman found it too awkward to not complete the motion of his hands and ended up completing the salute. Not without a grimace peeking out behind his handlebar moustache. Frankly the doormen at Delhi's five - star hotels would make the best tax sleuths in the country. They did not need to see tax returns to estimate income and wealth figures of whoever crossed their sight. Ultimately, the grandeur of the salute had a direct correlation to the size of the tip which many handed out to the doormen. Without doubt, the doorman had made up his mind looking at Vikas that the eventual tip would be non-existent. And perhaps rightly so.

It's not that Vikas looked disreputable. It was just the combination of the greenish brown panting Maruti 1000 and Vikas's slightly harried look that made the gateman wonder whether he was a bona fide visitor or not.

Of course, he was. Invited for lunch by Magnus Montgomery in the sprawling lawns of the Taj Palace. A table was specially set up a good ten cricket pitch-lengths away from the other tables under the protective cream coloured patio. The only common factor among each of the tables was the presence of at least one *gora* or *gori*. Who else could afford this luxury on a weekday at eleven in the morning thought Vikas. Not entirely accurate, but that was the drift of Vikas's thoughts.

Vikas had taken care to shovel out all facial hair from his pinkish facial features and had tried his best to apply copious amounts of oil to keep his wavy hair from going astray. Just as he was leaving his paternal home in Rajouri Gardens, his mother had smudged a little bit of *kajal* from her eye liner on his forehead. All the way from Rajouri Gardens to the Taj Palace, at every red flight Vikas would try to bring to the foreground a few strands of hair to cover the black dot. After all it was not auspicious to rub out the *nazar ka tika*.

He had no idea why Magnus had called him for lunch. He knew lightning would not strike at the same place twice. The fees that he had pocketed from Magnus last time was beyond his wildest imagination. It had opened up a lucrative stream of work for him. What more could he ask for? *Khao pio aur khisko.*

Vikas's life was about to change in ways he could not have even dreamt off. If the journey from the government quarters in Rajouri Gardens, home to his postal service lower division clerk father to Jor Bagh, home to the Ambassador of

Netherlands was beyond belief, the story was just about to get stranger.

"So Vikas, how are you?" said a pin-striped suit clad Magnus minus the red tie he had seen last time.

"Fine, Mr. Montgomery. How are you?"

"Clutching my passport for dear life," laughed Magnus patting the breast pocket of his gray pin-striped suit. Magnus had flawless cheeks. No facial hair. No pimples. Only two perfectly placed dimples which appeared every time he smiled. His hair was perfectly back brushed with a lot of gel. Unlike Vikas's Keokarpin hair oil, this was odourless completely.

Magnus ensured that wherever his travels took him, he made time for at least thirty minutes on the treadmill of the hotel gym. And it showed. All those cholesterol laden meals immersed in alcohol of various hues did make a dent in the mid-section of his five -foot nine- inch frame, but not by much. Vikas had been having *paneer pakodas* from the stall in the West Punjabi Bagh market a couple of times every week to balance the healthy diet that he and his father were dished out by his mother for lunch and dinner every day. Vikas at one point was very keen on the gym in Janakpuri, which had an attractive name *The Janak Body*. But the upfront membership fees could only be afforded by those whose bodies were beyond repair! So, he made sure he did some *daand baithaks* on the gray cement floor of his room in the hope at least the fat of one *pakoda* would melt per touchdown.

Once Vikas and Magnus were done sizing up each other's physical fitness levels or the lack thereof, Magnus broke the ice, "So, how is business Vikas?"

"Business has been rather good, Mr. Montgomery."

"Just call me Magnus please. Being called Mr. Montgomery by someone not too young makes me feel weird."

"Sure Magnus."

"I don't know how much you know about Banque Privee Wedderburn and the work I do on the Indian Sub-Continent but let me explain for absolute clarity. Our bank was set up in Lausanne in 1789 and has since catered to wealth management requirements of globally affluent families since then. I joined the bank about twenty years ago and have focussed on growing the business in India, Pakistan and Singapore."

Vikas had known of ICICI Bank which had opened a branch in West Punjabi Bagh market with great fanfare. To cater to the horny shopkeeper population, the local branch manager had ensured that Mandira Bedi in a noodle strap had landed up for the ribbon cutting ceremony. For a while, people had thought that ICICI Bank was a foreign bank, but soon it matched the Punjab and Sind Bank which had an incumbent advantage in West Delhi rupee for rupee. In service. In timelines. In queues. In everything on the lower scale of service standards.

Vikas just could not understand where this bank was and what exactly it did.

Magnus guessed the thoughts on Vikas's mind immediately. Magnus explained that Banque Privee Wedderburn was established about two hundred years ago in Lausanne in Switzerland. He then explained that many rich Indians, Pakistanis and Singaporeans had bank accounts there. A slight knowing smile spread along the sides of Magnus's pink cheeks growing gently into his dimples. Vikas's concept of banking was just about to be transformed.

"You mean people in Delhi have accounts in your bank in Laussane?"

"Not just from Delhi, but Lucknow, Amritsar, Coimbatore, Bangalore, Calcutta and many other places."

"And how do they operate such accounts?"

"Vikas, these amounts are invested in overseas stock exchanges and bond markets or sometimes just held in cash deposits."

Vikas had heard of the Bombay Stock Exchange and even the Delhi Stock Exchange, but to imagine a bank in far away in a town he had never heard off investing in foreign stock markets was too much. Surely this guy was a fraud. He was thinking about his customer base in West Punjabi Bagh. Would they keep money in a bank in an unheard off town in Switzerland when ICICI Bank was next door?

Vikas's mouth probably had by now opened wide enough for a squadron of flies to enter. Very gradually, he started to understand internally how this system worked. Here he was a Delhi-ite for life scrapping around visas and passports of foreigners for a living and here was a *firang* taking deposits from other *Delhiwalas* in Zurich. Classical fairness in his life.

Magnus thanked him profusely over lunch for being so proactive in getting his visa renewal sorted the last time around. And then he got to the point.

9.

When Vikas entered the armpit of India in Moradabad in his still sputtering Maruti 1000, he was thoroughly taken in by the town. Suburban towns fascinated Vikas. Possibly he was the only one in that place at any point in time to be fascinated. Surely none of the lumpens hanging around in the sprawling Company Bagh in the heart of Moradabad had anything but disgust or long - suffering feelings of resignation about the city. The former emotion was likely to be more prevalent.

He was to find an address in *Peetal Mandi*. He stopped at a shop and struck up a conversation over a semi-cold Thums Up. With the directions in his mind and the Thums Up having quenched his thirst of the four - hour drive from Delhi, Vikas set off on foot towards the largest bronze ware market in Asia.

Some shops had numbers, others did not. It was a bit of a guessing game to get to the right number. Mostly shops went by their owner's names. There turned out to be two Pradhans. One Pradhan stocked brass statuettes and the other candle ware. The statuettes were sold by a bald red *tilak* bearing rotund gent who was so grotesquely scratching his crotch over his once white pyjama that Vikas did not feel like pursuing the conversation any further.

It was not that Vikas had anything against scratching one's crotch in public. It was just the combination of the looks of the elderly Pradhan with his vigorous and frequent hand movements that disgusted Vikas.

When he finally entered the other Pradhan shop, he saw yet another sight he had never seen before in *Peetal Mandi* at least. He saw Rishika Pradhan's back clad in a maroon and green *salwar kameez* taking down a cardboard box from a shelf while standing on a rickety steel chair. He knew that the rickety chair toppled over only in Hindi films and did not pin any silly hopes on that eventuality.

Rishika Pradhan from behind was a work of art. The way Rishika's hair fell over her shoulder. The way the *salwar kameez* down till her buttocks was filled out just enough to ignite Vikas's desire to see her from the front. Not that West Punjabi Bagh or Rajouri Garden had any dearth of well filled out women, but there was something about the way Rishika's waist length hair gently caressed the globes of her behind leaving a lot to imagination. A lot to imagine. Essentially, how the scene would look minus the minor irritant of the maroon and green *salwar kameez*. Just as Vikas in his mind's eye was peeling off the *nada* of Rishika's *salwar* having successfully dislodged the *kameez* a while ago, she disembarked from the chair and turned around.

"*Haanji bataaiye,*" Rishika sought to know without even looking up at Vikas and setting down the cardboard box on the counter that separated her and Vikas's lustful mental machinations.

"Order *dena tha,*" managed Vikas taking in Rishika's frontage and syncing it mentally where his thought process was abruptly interrupted when she got down from her perch. Rishika's front was equally if not more spectacular than her behind. Milky white skin, the sort that daily intake of saffron and *haldi wala doodh* from when she was a few months old till date would have induced. Her cheekbones though wide were well filled out yet again, in the way where just another spoonful of *ghee* would make them obese. But in their present form would together with her heavy breasts qualify as *dasha* which his Bengali neighbour in West Punjabi Bagh had once told him meant ripe enough to pick and sample. What a delight it would be to sample her thought Vikas.

"*Dijiye*," responded Rishika and locked her eyes with Vikas. Vikas's two- day old stubble on his fair jowls gave him a lot of confidence. A bit akin to the Marlboro man. He self - consciously ruffled his jet- black hair front to back for no apparent reason. Then his hands went straight back into the side pockets of his Aslam Darzi stitched khakhi brown trousers as if looking for some scraps of paper. None were found.

Rishika raised her eyebrows and reiterated herself, "*Dijiye*."

"Indian Idol," sputtered out Vikas.

"Why have you come to *Peetal Mandi* if you want to apply for the Indian Idol?" sought to know Rishika.

He didn't look the *lukha* sort and she strangely felt no discomfort meeting his gaze. A rarity in Moradabad and more so in the Mohameddan by lanes of *Peetal Mandi*. For many years she thought the lane was called Mohammedan because every shop owner or worker inevitably carried the name Mohammed at the front, back or middle of their names. In fact, some were so closely identified with Mohammed that they had neither a prefix nor a suffix.

The guy in front of her did not seem to be from the Mohammeddan by lane or from *Peetal Mandi* either. Maybe he had come from Rampur. There was joke in her college on how Rampuri men had a certain swagger and style about them, which anyone but them found to be innately comical. In her quick 10 micro -second assessment, Rishika had three words to describe Vikas in her mind's eye: *bhola*, *sharif* and *thoda budhu*. If only she had a way to tune into Vikas's thoughts from the time he had entered her shop!

"I needed to place an order for idols. *Peetal wale.*"

"Bhaisahab, *Peetal Mandi mein sone chandi ke* idol *to milenge nahin.* But in any event, you have come to the wrong shop. There is another shop run by Devdutt Pradhan which is three lanes away. Just ask and someone or the other will show you. And avoid going through the *Mohameddan Gali*."

The last sentence was added almost as a statutory warning was bolted onto a pack of cigarettes. No one realised they had said it. Yet they had said it. From the time Rishika had been six years old, she used to remember anyone and everyone giving directions to anyone and everyone adding that statutory warning pithily. Anyone and everyone within her family and her father's business circle that is.

Vikas had no desire to go back to that ugly hulk of a crotch scratching man as Rishika was directing him to. He persisted, "You see, I am in a hurry. Can you take my order? I will give you an advance and collect these items from you. You can take a cut over and above the price that Devdutt Pradhan charges you."

"*Rampuriya lagte ho*. What do you think? I am your personal assistant that I will go around running errands for you. *Sasuraal mein aaye ho*."

Vikas took that last line meant in derision as some sort of initial interest. By this time Rakesh Pradhan had come back to the shop from one of the many workshops in the *Mohameddan Gali*. Vikas could immediately see the resemblance between father and daughter. The same expression commencing around the edge of the eyes culminating onto the chin, which could as easily break into a smile or shrink into a grimace. In this case Rakesh Pradhan's expression was anything but jovial.

"*Haanji*, what can we do for you?"

"I just needed some brass idols ordered and wondered, if you could co-ordinate this for me, as I have to return to Delhi tonight."

"You have come all the way from Delhi?"

"*Ji*," offered Vikas wondering what that had to do with his request.

"*Papa*, he wants us to obtain idols from Devdutt Ji's shop and deliver to him," intervened Rishika.

"How many pieces?" sought to know Rakesh Pradhan.

"2000."

"We will do it. Give us an advance of fifty thousand rupees."

Vikas quickly withdraw a thick wad of notes from his satchel and handed it over to Rakesh Pradhan. All he could imagine was when and if he would leave the shop and he could commence his conversations with Rishika. That was not to happen.

Once Rakesh Pradhan had arrived and had surveyed and concluded that Vikas was exactly the sort of person who any father would want to keep away a young nubile daughter from, he was not going to budge. So questioning was the way to best way to thwart Vikas's intentions. Actually, it was nothing personal against Vikas. The Pradhan couple would have treated every man the same way if they saw them interacting with Rishika.

"So, why do you need so many brass items?"

"I give it as gifts to clients."

"What type of clients?"

"I have a travel agency in Delhi."

"Where in Delhi?"

Behanchod tujhe kya was the response that Vikas found building up in his throat and Rakesh Pradhan was left in no doubt about it either. But nothing was said further, because Rishika had returned from the anterior of the shop with two glasses of rhododendron red *Roohafza*. Vikas quickly extended his hand to pick up the tall copper glass.

"You have all food and drink in copper glasses?" Vikas ventured to make conversation.

"*Haan aapke tarah sone chandi ke palang pe to sote nahin hai hum,*" curtly interjected Rishika.

Vikas was loving this girl every minute. Every time she stood up, he surreptitiously took a peek at her healthy thighs which rounded up just perfectly at her hips. Together with her alluring body, it was her manner of speaking that Vikas found winning. Not really. Who was he kidding. After years of watching awesome Punjabi girls turn into horribly *phaili huyi* aunties in West Punjbai Bagh and the surroundings – basically from *rasmalai* to *raita* he was beginning to understand that Rishika was ethereal. Ya right *tharak ke pujari* came his inner voice right back almost bringing a smirk to his face.

And so, the dye was cast. Vikas was totally and irrevocably smitten by Rishika. All he could think about was ways and means to get to talk more with her without the overhang of her pesky father. On her part, Rishika quite enjoyed the interaction as well, having had to deal with far more aggressive loutish youth in Peetal Mandi and in her college. In a way the fact that he allowed her to win in her game of one upmanship endeared him to her immeasurably.

10.

The entire community of bachelor men and most other unworthies in Moradabad had termed Rishika as a *naade ki* tight *laundiya* meaning not one to slip on the charms of the local lads or one who held out for an outside prince charming to arrive. So, when Vikas had first met Rishika at her father's shop in *Peetal Mandi* something about that interaction had penetrated her heart. Enough for her to have sought out further meetings, which always were initiated by Vikas. Even when a few phone calls would have sorted out a matter in *Peetal Mandi*, he would insist on coming down to Moradabad. Those were the days when Rishika always had extra classes or *saheli ke ghar ke* visits.

On one of those visits, she had pretended to be naïve and wanted to see the inside of Vikas's room at the Amara Boutique Hotel in Civil Lines. By then on Magnus' instructions, Vikas was enabling the collection and transfer of literally truckloads of cash from various parts of India through Tyagiji's *hawala* parlour in West Punjabi Bagh.

For cash collected within Delhi, taking it to Tyagiji's shop was easy peasy in Vikas's old Maruti 1000. It was when it was collected from Jaipur, Lucknow, Chandigarh and Shimla that all the *Peetal Mandi* wares were jam packed into the back seat of Vikas's car. Inevitably he was stopped at state borders, and he had acquired a reputation among the state police border constables of being a generous trader of copper ware.

He inevitably ended up giving out a few copper candlestands or other items which he procured at the lowest possible cost in Moradabad. He allowed full inspection of the seats and boot. The constables so enamoured with the tons of copper ware which they assumed he wanted to evade octroi by transferring in his car, never once opened his suitcases. Not once. Not once in over five years of being Magnus' money mule.

Why on earth did they need to delve into his personal *chaddi*, *baniyan* and *taulia* when better wares presented themselves? Very soon across state borders, small shops selling *Peetal Mandi* wares sprung up, which Vikas always chuckled at when crossing them with millions of dollars or rupees in suitcases loosely strewn around. Really old suitcases. No one wanted to take them!

So, with these activities going on, Vikas's monthly income had gone up several notches and Magnus was always generous in plying him with a fair bit of spending money. So, when Vikas had booked himself into Moradabad's finest hotel, he had harboured a flimsy hope that somehow Rishika would come inside. It didn't happen the first six times or so. And then it did.

So, when Rishika lay inside the exquisitely laid out bed, having gifted her virginity to Vikas, there was a faint smile on her face.

"Ho hi gaya," ventured Rishika.

"Rukna mushkil hi nahin namumkin tha," came the spent Vikas's response.

"Ab tumhe lag raha hoga main shaadi ke liye chep ho jaungi."

"Nahin. Iske baad to main chep ho jaunga."

"Sochna bhi mat."

There was something about cheesy dialogues from the dark decades of Bollywood that welded the minds of Rishika and Vikas. They just loved picking up apt sentences randomly from different movies and using it on each other. The hundreds of hours that Rishika used to spend before her stereo set trying to record Bollywood songs onto cassettes and then labelling them were finally being used with an equal match. And since cassettes were in short supply, after a while she had to erase some songs and re-record on top of them.

The stereo and the video cassette recorder were her lifeline. Somehow after meeting Vikas who matched her dirty dialogue for dirty dialogue, suggestive stanza for suggestive stanza, suddenly she began to see a retrospective divine intervention in cultivating her passion for Bollywood. Vikas had exactly the same set of equipment in his father's cramped flat in Rajouri Gardens and pretty much the same fascination for all things Bollywood.

That night Rishika had sat on the terrace of her house in one corner with her back to the greenish black wall in her loose salwar kameez. The grin refused to leave her jowls. The grin was becoming more of a smirk as she replayed the entire chain of events that unfolded with Vikas a mere few hours ago. She could spend her entire life with Vikas like that. Intertwined in passive ecstasy. At total peace. All the tension that was building up over all his visits in the last few months and their consequent phone conversations now taken to their logical conclusion.

It was the conversational lucidity between them. So *filmy* and yet so heartfelt. Every sentence met another one perfectly timed taken from a different context but matched the tenor of the first seamlessly.

11.

Banque Wedderburn Privee faced a massive penalty from the US Department of Justice which saw almost all accrued reserves disappear into the ether. As with any crisis within any industry this presented the perfect solution for the consulting industry to slice off some further revenues. Actually, not just some revenues. After taking off their fees, unless the bank implemented their solution, the shareholders might have had to sign up for a cash counting role at Hell – one of Zurich's happening casino cum night club.

Offshoring the back office became a buzzword in Swiss banking. The head honchos were at odds to reconcile Swiss banking secrecy with offshoring key client information. Ultimately the powers that be bit the bullet and created an elaborate maze of codes which only someone inside the Swiss vault could de-code. So, the back office received numbers and figures, but no iota of client identification details.

Quite obviously, in the above climate, India presented itself as a beacon of hope. A few vendors were invited to bid for this piece of work and given the codes in place, Banque Wedderburn Privee contracted New Horizon Infotech Limited in Noida to carry out routine back - office operations.

In this backdrop when Rishika Pradhan came looking for a job to Vikas, he pointed her in this direction having had gathered these details from Magnus. The promoters of New Horizon were only too happy to accommodate Rishika in the operations team supporting Banque Wedderburn Privee.

Böök IV

Thë Nëw Bëginning (1992-2000)

1. Zurich - The Ascent

Vikas Kumar crossed the Bucherer everyday while going back and forth between his office near Pelikanstrasse and the rail station at Bahnhofstrasse. Unlike others who stared wide eyed at the glass windows of one of the world's most famous jewellery shops, Vikas strangely found great emotional succour at its mere sight.

The windows decked with some of the most expensive watches and jewels in the world, reminded him in fair measure of the life he had left behind in West Punjabi Bagh. So similar in the presentation of their wares to the world, just like Khanna Jewellers who occupied pride of place in the Main Market of West Punjabi Bagh.

The strange twist in fortune that had catapulted him from a tiny cubbyhole of a shop in West Punjabi Bagh to the mysterious wood panelled private banking backrooms of Banque Wedderburn Privee in Zurich. Four years in Zurich had taught him that only what one could never contemplate would always happen.

Who could have thought he would have a miraculous career change from being a travel arranger in West Punjabi Bagh to a private banker in Zurich. It was not even a career change it was a career transplant. He still remembered how astonished he had first been to learn of people let alone in West Punjabi Bagh, but places as far out as Saharanpur and Virbhadra who had bank accounts in Zurich. Now he managed several of those offshore bank accounts.

The girl who he loved so much in Moradabad now lived with him in Zurich. As his lawfully wedded wife. From being the wife of a travel agent in West Punjabi Bagh who ran errands for wealthy clients of Banque Wedderburn Privee, she had now come to become the wife of an Executive Director of Zurich's elite private bank. All thanks to a freak ski accident.

A freak ski accident of a high rolling private banker who managed the book of very wealthy Indian clients with offshore bank accounts. A book so highly secretive with numbers that the transitional manger could only locate sketchy details of a Vikas Kumar. The same Vikas Kumar who seemed to be the local henchman of Magnus Montgomery. That is where the trail of the actual clients went cold.

The bank had long been concerned about the highly individualistic style of Magnus Montgomery. It had at various points tried to institutionalise the business brought in by him. With no success at all. Magnus ran his own parallel shop within the bank. A bank with Chinese walls with the rest of the bank. He often joked that he paid extortionate rent to the bank in terms of the revenue he brought in, and they should just let him be. Whilst the bank was paranoid at the breach of protocols and policies all around, the potential loss of revenue from a revolt by Magnus left them helpless. Till such time as the inevitable happened.

When Magnus had a freak ski accident on the slopes of Cervinia which threw him into coma, the bank was desperate not to let it impact the business. That's when the wheels of Vikas's fortune turned. And what a turn of the wheel it was. Far more exhilarating and potentially more coma inducing than even Magnus's deceleration into coma on the alpine slopes.

In order to save, serve and potentially institutionalise this book of clients, while Magnus was indisposed, the transitional manger was flown down to Delhi to track down Vikas. And to bring him back to Zurich within four weeks start to finish to ensure that client service was not impacted. What served the bank well was that Vikas had met almost seventy per cent of the clients that Magnus had looked after over the last several years.

The transitional manager had a clear brief - get all client contact details from Vikas and rescue the book of clients.

Vikas of course had other ideas when he realised the gravity of the situation. He initially thought he could manage the clients by staying in India, but the transitional manager armed with a legal opinion from Jayant Dada Thatte of the Bombay High Court put such ideas to rest. So Vikas' *ruksat* as they would have said in his *sasural* in Moradabad happened quicker than he could find a replacement for his now flourishing travel agency.

Landing in Zurich with no idea of either the country or the role he was to perform strangely did not unnerve Vikas. He was there for the ride. That too on a free ticket. When he flew business class as was the norm for private bankers of Banque Wedderburn Privee from Delhi to Zurich on Swiss Air, he marvelled at the wonders of life.

From driving a ramshackle Maruti 1000 between Delhi and Moradabad and booking tons of airline tickets, he was actually being served in the business class of Swiss Air. He had hurriedly bought a few formal clothes from the West Punjabi Bagh designer shops, little knowing that Swiss bankers dressed very differently from a Punjabi wedding party *baraat*.

Zurich. Zurich. Zurich. Every pore of Vikas's body was absorbed by the enormity of the beauty before him. Not of Zurich. But of Luschner. A buxom white lady in a black tight dress embellishing every curve who had arrived to pick him up from the Zurich Airport. Crisp, business-like and yet a warmth which permeated her every utterance. A warmth which was challenging Vikas's marriage vows during the half hour car ride between the Zurich Airport and his serviced apartment in Albisrieden.

He figured out that Luschner was the Head of Human Resources at the bank and was there to ensure his integration into the bank's culture and help him settle in personally. Only later did he fathom that the entire Human Resources function at the bank was the sum total of one, comprising Luschner alone. He was also to realise soon that the culture of private banking was brutal, with very little for Luschner to do. That is possibly why she took the day off to come and pick him up from the airport. Be that as it may, he enjoyed the ride.

2.

Notwithstanding the best of intentions on Luchner's behalf, Vikas's integration into the bank was stormy to say the least. The Head of the Private Bank was a Swiss bloke, Javier Martin who ran a tight ship. By the time, he had realised that the relevant Market Head had sanctioned a downright rookie to join the ranks of the bank, Vikas was well entrenched within the headquarters of Bank Wedderburn Privee at Pelikanstrasse.

Well entrenched because he had now matched some of the numbered accounts against the contact details he had in his green diary. Only some. There were still a few accounts, which he could not make head or tail of in terms of identity of the ultimate beneficial owners or in plain English, the account holders.

The private banking assistants who used to man Magnus Montgomery's office phone had beady instructions to pass on calls from any and all customers to Vikas. That yielded a few more hits but some more accounts remained shrouded in the well-deserved secrecy that a Swiss private banking relationship demanded. A few times the actual customers or their authorised signatories landed up at the doorsteps of the bank in Zurich and that helped solve some other pieces. With every discovery, Vikas gradually was metamorphosing from a travel agent to a consummate private banker. Having learnt his craft with hard - nosed businessmen of West Punjabi Bagh, eking out a margin for himself, howsoever small came as second nature to him.

So, once he understood the levers of the game in Zurich, he was soon able to ensure that the customers were fairly charged for all private banking services they sought. Also, given the services he had performed for many of them on instructions from Magnus, he knew the exact source of where the money came from. More than that he also knew the exact neural pathways of the transformation of the bags of cash he lugged across states in India into ledger entries at Banque Wedderburn Privee. That gave him supreme awareness of the jugular veins of such clients.

Vikas figured out the basics of the job early on. To ensure that account balances across the accounts handed over to him crept north and wherever possible locked into some investments which made exit of the same funds unattractive or impossible. The bank's credo was clear to Vikas.

The bank took other people's money and applied their experience to it. Experience of investments, experience of structuring, experience of avoiding bad experiences. After a while the bank had the money and the customer experienced it at a distance. Some in the form of bank statements. Some who only wanted in - person meetings in the privacy of their homes in India. Some came over to Zurich *en route* their customary summer sojourns in London or other European havens.

3.

Mark Scharer was a lifer at Banque Wedderburn Privee. Starting out as a bean counter at the ripe young age of twenty - two, he was now a Managing Director and Market Head for South - East Asia. Being the most profitable business group within the bank, he was also a part of the bank's Executive Committee. Mark had been instrumental in luring Magnus Montgomery from a much larger rival.

Magnus' move had yielded the bank over five billion Swiss francs worth of assets under management. In other words, that was the amount of hard cash that moved into the coffers and vaults of Banque Wedderburn Privee. That was the reward.

Soon, Mark had comprehended the cost of the prize catch. He had to hand over complete and total autonomy to Magnus. In spite of repeated warnings from other members of the Executive Committee about the non-institutionalised nature of Magnus' business, Mark chose to remain mum. Remain mum till there was an opening. An opening to figure out a way to get his hands around the book of clients that Magnus carried with him.

Magnus Montgomery did not keep client details in the office. He did not file trip notes. He did not file expense reports. He bulldozed over whatever processes that applied to everyone else in the bank. This was his way of keeping the clients secure only to himself. His assistants only knew clients by numbers and alphabets. Investments for clients again were done through the bank's own funds and any and all reconciliation was carried out by Magnus. Only he and his clients knew what was happening to their money. Sometimes even the clients did not know. Such was the level of trust Magnus commanded among his clients. They happily handed over discretionary mandates to Magnus at wildly exorbitant fees to invest their monies as he saw fit. No questions asked. Magnus never failed to deliver. In many cases, as Vikas later found out, any surplus income generated on the principal deposit amount was a bonus for the clients. Many were just happy to have the secrecy wrapper around the funds deposited in Switzerland within the coffers of Banque Wedderburn Privee.

Mark realised early on in Magnus's tenure that it would be counter-productive to the profitability of his region to force him into the bank's mould. He gave him a free hand and glossed over process failures at Executive Committee meetings using the large fig leaves offered by the revenue figures that Magnus contributed to. The revenue generated by Magnus was the highest not just within this bank, but also among all of the bankers who did similar business in Zurich. Not just in Zurich actually. Very possibly in all of Switzerland.

Obviously, Mark was certain that many other banks routinely courted Magnus and money alone would never be enough to keep Magnus stuck to this bank. Magnus demanded complete sovereignty from the bank and in turn returned absolute secrecy to his clients.

Magnus did not have any family that the bank was aware of. He of course did not fill out any of the questionnaires duly circulated by Luschner from Human Resources when he came into the bank. His residential address was unknown to the bank. When he left the bank for client visits or business trips, he merely trooped in and picked up wads of petty cash from the bank's cashier and signed off a tiny scrap of paper. That was about the only record the bank could get him to sign.

So, when Magnus went missing from duty for over three weeks, Mark was not unduly worried. Magnus was known to visit India for weeks on end. Of course, his prudence and temerity prevented any further inquiry or investigation into the purpose. Once six weeks had passed, Mark did not have to worry any more.

A call had come in from the Lausanne University Hospital. Given the gravity of the situation Magnus' assistant had passed on the call to Mark. That's when the enormity of the task ahead for Mark to ring-fence and rescue such a profitable business hit him. Secretly, he also let a thought persist in the corner of his mind, which lingered in relation to finally being able to institutionalise this part of the business. Not for long though.

Having ransacked Magnus's office himself and with the help of two junior bankers, who thought they would inherit the clients whose details were minutes away from discovery, Mark's blood pressure hit a new high. Because nothing but a few platinum entry cards for gentlemen's clubs in Zurich were found. In particular, the buxom blonde on the glitzy card titled Hell caught Mark's attention. The way that card was designed, if he turned it over, he could see the posterior of the buxom blonde from the frontage. Of course, naked on both ends. That's exactly how Mark felt at that moment. Naked before the Executive Committee for having glossed over processes, when this was exactly the eventuality that they had predicted.

Having served the bank for over twenty years, Mark now shuddered at the prospect of having to perhaps visit all of these houses of ill repute to unearth any clues about the client book that Magnus served. For years, he had been warned about such an eventuality and for years he had made excuses about not wanting to rock the boat when the going was good. Finally, the tide had turned. And he was found sleeping at the wheel. Sleeping totally naked. The mere thought of not being able to find five billion Swiss francs worth of client monies made him want to throw up.

While Magnus slept a pre-birth like sleep in an Intensive Care Unit at the Lausanne University Hospital, sleep permanently wiped out from Mark's existence. Minus the revenue generated from Magnus' book of clients, he might as well have joined the ranks of the junior private bankers. That worried him sufficiently to have not even sought the details of what had put Magnus into coma. When he spoke to a transitional manager within the bank about finding clues from bank reconciliations as to the identity and contact details of the Indian clients, he had a rude shock awaiting him.

Apparently, Magnus used to physically obtain records of bank transfers into his portfolio accounts and ensure they never formed part of the bank's documentary records. This flagrant breach of bank protocols had been flagged up to him, but he had never found it apt to intervene.

So, what was Mark left with? A senior private banker in coma. Actually, the star of the private banking world of Zurich - the *Badshah of Zurich was* in coma and the Sultanate suddenly seemed vulnerable. No client details whatsoever. While he fiddled with the platinum gilt edged entry card for Hell, he wondered if this is how his career was destined to end. His mind flickered onto Magnus' choice at those gentlemen's clubs for a stray second only to come back into focus. Focus onto the task at hand. The task which had no end in sight. Only a beginning.

4.

Mark Scharer constituted a committee led by a transitional manager, drawn from the ranks of the Operations team at Banque Wedderburn Privee to make headway into the identity of the clients handled by Magnus Montgomery.

Mark felt he could save his scalp by having this committee produce a report highlighting significant operations failures which needed to be reinforced bank wide. Who knows he may even get a pay rise if the Executive Committee adopted this report bank wide. Who knows even pigs could fly one day. One day.

The transitional manager, Jeremy Franks was an ambitious career Operations man, who detested the high - handed ways of bankers like Magnus. More than that he hated deft corporate manoeuvres such as the one executed by Mark. Which made him start looking for disparate strands of information in vacuum.

Still, he knew if Magnus had the clients, he would find them. He would find them for the bank. He would find them for himself. He would find them to show the likes of Mark who the boss was. He would find them in full view of the Executive Committee so that no one was left in any doubt about the true saviour of this business. And in return he would transition from his drab Operations role to a frontline private banker. Who knows he could even get that yummy ass assistant in the post room to be his own personal assistant. Oh! those assets could finally be his. His to own to the exclusion of all others.

Jeremy whilst driven to save the business for entirely different reasons from that of Mark, was joint at the hip in terms of the end-goal. Who got the coveted prize was material, but unless the goal was reached neither would get anywhere close to where their respective imagination was taking them to. Mark for a moment imagined himself on the frontage of the glittering entry card to Hell totally naked around a silver pole. That is exactly how he would feel in front of the Executive Committee if this contagion was not contained, and sufficient comfort provided about the durability and sustainability of the business conducted by Magnus.

So, when Mark sanctioned Jeremy's business trip to India to follow a lead to uncover some of the clients, they both silently sighed. Praying for success of the mission, but at the same time plotting how to position themselves in the event Jeremy did succeed.

Having spent years in the Operations amidst datasheets and process charts, as opposed to Mark's schmoozing lunches, dinners and business class flights, Jeremy had a methodical approach to matters at hand.

Rather than hyperventilating after ransacking Magnus' room which yielded precious little as Mark did, Jeremy went about generating detailed bank statements of the numbered accounts in the hope the iterations could provide a clue. No clues there. He went about generating a schedule of all payments instructed by Magnus which went via the bank's payment gateways. Admittedly there were very few of those transactions.

Jeremy understood, why Magnus was so successful. He managed to gather large amounts of assets in terms of cash from his clients and it seemed very little or negligible amounts ever left the bank. He wondered about the sort of eventuality that these clients were gathering a war chest in a Swiss bank for. In some cases, for over seven years such minor amounts, if ever, left their accounts. Even when minor amounts left their bank accounts, they were replenished fairly soon in several multiples. Almost always in cash. Hard cash. The suitcase variety. Actually, many suitcases full of wads of cash. The sort of suitcases which Vikas seemed to have a great deal of familiarity with.

Jeremy wondered if Magnus had on his personal secret payroll a team of mules who lugged these wads of cash over the Hindukhush mountains which he had studied in geography class in school from India into the European mainland. He broke out of this vivid imagery in his mind when it became clear that the mule destined to do Mark's dirty work was him. Not for long though. He would show Mark who the real ninja was.

Böök V

Thë End öf thë Bëginning (1992–2002)

1. Brief Interlude in San Francisco: A Bench Overlooking the Justin Herman Plaza

Zainab Siddiqui flicked an obstinate curl behind her right ear. It refused to yield to her gesture. The gale winds coming from the San Francisco Bay over the Ferry Building felt like a sack of quinoa breaking over her white pashmina coat covered shoulders. Heavy on landing, yet strangely mellow in its impact. Much like the vortex of emotions breaking within her.

A pink scarf covered the nape of her neck just below where the white woollen cap should have ended. She was swirling the cap in her hand. It was all eerily different. The cap, the scarf, the pashmina coat. The slenderness of each of these items mirrored the shallowness of her relationships in San Francisco.

The comfort of her bulky red *rajai* in Virhbhadra was unmatched by the skinny duvet at her studio apartment in the heaven hugging Embarcadero Centre a few steps behind to where she was sitting. But that was not the point.

The point really was that she did not understand why her passport still had a spelling error in it. Whether the subtle difference in the spelling of her name or the subtle difference in the colour of her passport was more confounding she still could not make up her mind. The only time she had caught a fleeting glimpse of her navy-blue United States of America passport was during a mad dash trip to Muzzafarnagar to attend the last rites of her *khala*.

Zainab had calculated that the timing of her appearance at the *Salat al Janazah* was all of an hour compared to the seventeen-hour flight to Delhi and the roughly three-hour car ride to Muzzafarnagar. And before she had time to recover from the travel fatigue, she was back at the Indira Gandhi International Airport and ushered back into the Air India flight back to San Francisco. All the while her mother's words from their San Jose perch hung heavy and rang in her years, "*Beta*, just hug her one last time for me."

Zainab had wanted to know what urgency had prevented her mother from being able to travel. Equally, her father had sought to explain her chaperone at the San Francisco Airport who had brandished her passport at the check-in counter as an office colleague. The one who had arranged for her travel documents at the last minute. The same chaperone had magically appeared when the flight had touched down in Delhi and escorted her to a waiting car and whizzed off to Muzzafarnagar. Zainab did not even want to get into the nature of the supposed office that her father was attending to in San Jose. That was well and truly beyond what her delicate brain cells could process at this point.

Zainab was just not able to conjure up any material feelings of grief amidst the wailing and wheezing at the *Salat al Janazah* as these other thoughts just did not leave her mind. Till such time as her father's so-called office colleague tapped her shoulder and they made their journey back. No conversations. No names asked. No names told.

When her mother had rung her to tell her about the trip to Muzzafarnagar, Zainab's first thought was how she would get in touch with Varun Dixit. The Varun Dixit. The Varun Dixit who had refused any email correspondence with her. The Varun Dixit who had hurtled Zainab onto a revenge relationship spiral in San Francisco which refused to leave her. The Varun Dixit who just three years from the day could have thrown himself to a rabid mob if they had raised as much as an eyebrow on Zainab. But why would Zainab look for Varun in India? Didn't he say in his last email that he was in New Zealand, where his family had relocated? Didn't her father tell her that Varun had married a local girl to expedite his Kiwi citizenship?

Zainab's father had begged her with folded hands to not have any truck with Varun. Zainab had initially acquiesced, but her heart just could not fathom this turn of events. For the entire stay at the San Jose State University, Zainab hurtled from one man to another in the hope somehow the news would percolate to Varun. It never did.

Then Zainab went from one man to another in the hope of finding Varun in one of them. She never did. Till she did. And found love that she could not even imagine was possible.

Böök VI
Thë Bëginning öf thë Ënd (2002–2010)

1. Vikas & Rishika: The Lost Sultanate of Zurich

Vikas and Rishika's life had settled very quickly into a holy communion of domesticity in Zurich. You know the types. The type that includes getting on with love. None of the navel gazing or heady sex that defined its early avatar in Moradabad.

Vikas sometimes thought that the romance in that *haveli* in Moradabad could not ever be matched by what the Swiss Alps and the numerous alpine resorts they visited. For one the security and safety of the alpine resorts made making love unexciting, almost tepid. As opposed to the surreptitious forays in Moradabad where at every corner was a lurking eye or ear forever ready to carry back information about the *kaali kartoot* that he and Rishika were allegedly engaged in. Though nothing untoward ever happened, the fear of discovery, the thrill of the illicit encounters made it ever more adrenaline pumping.

When Rishika had hinted that he takes the step towards asking Rakesh Pradhan to formalise matters, he didn't flinch. After all, isn't that all he ever wanted? His travel agency business was doing well, though not because more travel arrangements were being made, but because he was now serving a lot of Banque Wedderburn Privee clients and being paid handsomely for his services by Magnus.

Aaja Baharon ki Mallika, Mausam Badal Jaye Dil Ka. And just how things changed post his holy matrimony with Rishika. He first got a deal to transfer over fifty million dollars from Delhi to Ras Al Khaima. The highest that Magnus had entrusted him with.

It was also a function of either defence procurement or election season in India. He tried not to bother with the cause behind the effect. He did as he was told. And he did it well. Covered all corners. Never cut any. Never put his own fingers in the till in spite of substantial opportunity at every stage. One of the clients had once told him that given that the monies they sent out to Banque Wedderburn Privee were essentially not declared for tax purposes in India, they almost accounted for a ten to twenty per cent leakage on the way. So, when the full amount showed up in the Swiss account, they were beyond surprised. This element alone had helped Vikas cement these relationships when Magnus slipped the ski slope and into coma.

Their honeymoon was at a resort in Ras Al Khaima during which time they sang, danced, and had sex on popular Bollywood ballads from the 1990s. The first two activities happened in the largely Indian music dominated dining room which had a live band every night belting out a medley of foot tapping and mind-numbing numbers. Back in their room, Rishika and Vikas could not help but replay these numbers and engage in their procreational activity. After all, in West Punjabi Bagh, the countdown to the kids started from the day after they returned from honeymoon. Rishika had told him the countdown was no different in Moradabad.

But one countdown was starkly different in Moradabad, which is why Rakesh Pradhan had heaved a sigh of relief on the seventh *phera* of Vikas and Rishika. Even though he suspected Rishika and Vikas of having exchanged bodily fluids prior to marriage, his fatherly *lakshamn rekha* prevented him from hectoring or lecturing any further on this point. The tag of *naade ki tight* was diametrically opposite to *uski bin biyahi* or in other words living together in sin. Actually, not living together in sin. A tad worse off. Screwing at will but with no prospect for marriage in sight. Moradabad obviously put a premium to fucking and the longer it was withheld till marriage the higher the premium.

So, when Rishika briefly worked at the New Horizon BPO on the recommendation of Magnus Montgomery, it was the most splendid part of their relationship. Rishika had no trouble smuggling in Vikas to fornicate at will at her Sector 47 high rise apartment in Noida. No moans were suppressed, no groans were muted. Quite rightly that development in Noida had been named Garden of Eden. The neighbours had not even started getting suspicious of this illicit liaison in their midst that marriage was announced. And that changed their sex life for good. Not for good. But for ever, for the worse.

Vikas's family home in Rajouri Gardens was the den of *mummyji* politics, where every move of the newly wed *dulhan* was closely scrutinised. Perhaps with more interest than the excise inspectors audited the account books in the adjoining industrial estate of Rohini. So, any public display of affection was frowned upon and given how closely the rooms were packed loud expressions of orgasmic pleasure were proscribed by the family constitution. Sex was only for the purpose of popping out a suitable *waris*. A male was a bonus. And it immeasurably altered the power equation of the *bahu* and in spite of long hours of labour, she would return with a visible spring in her step.

Rishika longed for her independence as the back-office executive of Baker Water Peter & Co at New Horizon. That was the word by which all documents of Banque Wedderburn Privee were encrypted. Rishika was perhaps the only employee on that account who knew or cared about the larger picture. The others were mighty content tapping in keys and routinely churning whatever tasks were given to them.

Actually, Rishika had zero interest in the backroom dealings of New Horizon or for that matter Banque Wedderburn Privee. She had very little interest in Vikas's work life and for her this job was good to escape Moradabad. But when the inevitable happened by way of the bank establishing contact with Vikas post Magnus's accident, he knew exactly how to ensure his value and Rishika dutifully played her part. A slap in the face of Swiss banking secrecy, but a solid feather in the cap for the new sultanate about to arise - the sultanate in Zurich of Rishika and Vikas – only this wasn't.

2.

The vagina forgets, but the heart remembers. Even after so many years of marriage with Rishika, that day of their illicit union in Moradabad remained his strongest memory. Whenever he thought of Rishika, the image of her milky white thighs drawn to her chest while he ploughed into her every orifice flashed before him. He could pin-point in his sleep the exact location of the three wonderfully placed moles on Rishika's blemish less bum.

Rishika was neither coy, nor a cowgirl the first time. It was as natural as natural could be. Vikas was neither gentle nor rough. They had this chemistry which did not make the act seem in any way sinful or unnatural. They blended from conversation to dialogue *baazi* to closely hugging and then disrobing slowly but in rhythm. A rhythm that was soothing as much to Rishika as it was to Vikas. It neither culminated in a toe-curling orgasm nor a prematurely ended session in pent up frustration. They both were satiated and spent and joined. Joined where they should be. From that point to here, something had come unstuck.

Was it merely Vikas's ambition of making the most of the chance at a private banking job in Zurich that was creating a ridge between them? Or was it to do with her inability to adjust to the way of life in Zurich? For someone who was closely ensconced in her mother's *pallu*, the move, first then to her *sasural* in Rajouri Gardens had been traumatic enough.

But there at least she got by because she could manage what her mother managed in Moradabad with the help of domestic help. Zurich was a totally different ball game. She did not understand the language and she did not get the rhythm of the city. And the direct impact of missing that rhythm was on her relationship with Vikas. While Vikas was expanding his universe within Banque Wedderburn Privee toppling account after hidden account and forging relationships with the richest Indian families, Rishika was withdrawing into a shell.

The shell first impacted her wanting to discover Switzerland. Whenever Vikas would collect intelligence about weekend getaways, Rishika rarely showed any enthusiasm. It's not that she was unhappy. She had just lost her verve. It would come back, but God knew when.

She was just not able to experience the happiness. Logically it all made sense, but she just was not able to get elated. She was much more at ease eating momos off a street side stall in West Punjabi Bagh market in the complex where Vikas had his travel agency. Money was not a constraint really there, but the shared joy of coming out of her in-law's shadow in Rajouri Gardens in an auto rickshaw to West Punjabi Bagh to draw out Vikas from his small cocoon was something else. Here in Zurich, there were no in-laws and yet Rishika did not feel like leaving the flat. She knew Vikas did his best to ensure her adjustment to the city was seamless. But even Vikas's best fell short of her minimum threshold. It is not that she was giving him a tough time. She just could not help herself.

3.

Vikas in his impeccable tuxedo stitched at the Cordon Le Boutique in Talhastrasse at a mildly impoverishing price walked into the Zurich Landes Museum, with a disinterested

Rishika Pradhan with a glazed look her eyes. Not the one induced by early sundowners before the party, but the one caused by extreme boredom and the lack of zest for living. Living the life that Vikas wanted to. Living the life that brought Vikas to life.

The West Punjabi Bagh *ka launda* Vikas found nothing more exhilarating than dancing with gay abandon on *Husn hai suhaana* inside the sanctum sanctorum of the Zurich Landes Museum. He ended up dancing with every lady and man of every orientation, but not Rishika. Because she was well too self-conscious to pitch up to the dance floor. It was not always so, but she detested living it up in Zurich.

As far as Vikas was concerned, this was where lady luck had smiled on him to bring him to this august gathering and had then taken away the essence of it via Rishika. A far cry from *mata ki chowkis* or *jagratas* in West Punjabi Bagh. But this is where life was a great equaliser. If he had the opportunity, he now severely lacked the wherewithal to enjoy. The wherewithal was Rishika and how she had checked out of his life in totality. A slow and gradual burn, now complete.

Vikas knew and Rishika understood that this would be the last Bollywood Ball for them as a couple. Neither could keep up the pretence any longer. It was over. Actually, it was over, the day Vikas and Rishika had landed up in Zurich to build a life. Actually, building a book of business or salvaging one was the last of Vikas's priorities when he had arrived in Zurich. All he was glad was the privacy that the city afforded him and Rishika. Not just in their home away from the noise and clutter and the crowd of his Rajouri Garden digs, but also the anonymity of the city. Where they could own the streets without being accosted by *buaji* from Tagore Gardens or Sarojini Nagar *wale mamaji*.

This was where their dream to walk the streets where Govinda and Karishma Kapoor had scandalised an entire generation of Swiss Germans and their ilk on *Sohna Kitna Sohna Hai* would have found fruition.

Build a life, they certainly did. Just not with each other. At least Rishika did not. Rather could not.

4.

In a parallel world in Mahua, Prakhar Solanki was getting ready to take off with his wife Sejal for Zurich. Prakhar was part of the Data Analytics team at Infoedge in Pune and had just secured a two-year contract from his company to work on-site at Nestle in Zurich running an integration project. Sejal was excited because outside of Pune and Baroda, her exposure to anywhere else was only via films. And Yash Raj and Barjatya were the only vehicles through which Sejal had seen the world. High on colour. Higher on romance. Not that her marriage lacked romance, it was just the Mahua variety. A strangely plateaued relationship high on stability and sex, but low on potential.

Potential for what even Sejal did not know. She had stopped thinking ever since her all-Gujarat rank in the high school exams had shocked her parents into delaying her marriage. That was a shock to the social ecosystem in Mahua. Since that meant she got a scholarship to study for free under the Mukhya Mantri Balika Ayojna at the Mahua Inter College. Howsoever, as socially interconnected Sejal's father had been, he was not going to bring disrepute to his Gujarati roots by giving up something that came for free. Sejal realised early on in the college that she lacked the traditional Gujarati damsel looks. The types that testosterone laden undereducated and unemployed Gujarati male teens dreamed of defiling during the Navratras.

The college degree proved useful since instead of being married into the steel foundry family in Mahua as was the route for her schoolmates, she was picked up by an IT professional. Thus, at least Sejal got to get to Pune and commence her married life. It seemed like she had maxed out her potential till such time as Zurich happened.

In Zurich, Sejal found a world within her reach and grasp both. The complete and total freedom meant she was applying for jobs, meeting recruiters, getting more confidence in her Gujarati laden English and ended up as a Marketing Assistant at Banque Wedderburn Privee. The fact that it coincided with the lowest point in Vikas and Rishika's marriage was only the initial fuel to the fire.

Though Vikas's role at Banque Wedderburn Privee had no functional overlap with that of Sejal, disasters were cooked by the Almighty with a lot of care. Every manner of interaction was made possible for Vikas and Sejal to interact. When Banque Wedderburn Privee threw a bash for its clients at the Uto Kulm Hotel in Uetliberg to celebrate its 200th year of existence, Sejal was put in charge of chartering a special train to take the guests from Zurich HB rail station to Uetliberg. A special private train with a red carpet welcome and the finest champagne that money could buy.

Vikas did not look forward to such events. Not many of his clients attended such events and he merely had to tick mark his presence because of the three-line whip from the management. Vikas had heard of Magnus' non-co-operation with management and getting away with it, but his disposition was very different. Sejal's work was pretty much over when the last of the guests had seamlessly trooped up the last mile from the Uetliberg station to the banquet room of the Uto Kulm Hotel. Thereon, another marketing assistant was in-charge of the relay for the evening.

When Vikas and Sejal got talking, it was boring small shit. Nothing of consequence. They promised to catch up for a coffee someday. Vikas gave Sejal some tips on where to stock up on Indian groceries given her recent arrival. When Sejal turned around, Vikas instinctively glanced at her derriere but was soon consumed by other thoughts. Thoughts about what was more unpleasant. Staying on for the evening at this god forsaken event or going home to nothingness. He decided to stick on and for a reason unknown to him hoped that Sejal would be back for her marketing duties. And she did.

The expensive prosecco made conversation easier. Sejal who had never had much alcohol pre-Zurich was now a pro at swirling wines in glasses, sniffing them and "hmming" something inane about its qualities. Vikas commented about how quickly she had learnt and made a wry comment about how he wished his wife would adapt as quickly.

Sejal registered the comment but said nothing. It was part of the potential. For another time, another day. Or maybe never. Who knows. Zurich didn't happen by accident to her. Or did it. Anyhow the prosecco was loosening her tongue and she said something about the food being quite unappetising. Vikas remarked that she could have altered its course. Really? Sejal thought that she could not alter the course of anything in her life so far. It was first her parents and then Prakhar, who determined its direction. She mumbled something about being an assistant and not a Managing Director.

Vikas found it amusing and assumed that she knew nothing about his illustrious Rajouri Gardens-West Punjabi Bagh roots. Since Banque Wedderburn Privee had weathered the storm of his entry and stabilisation, the coffee-corner gossip about his acceptability had died down. Not that he was one of their own. That Vikas knew, he never would be. But as a revenue earner he was certainly at the core of the management's thinking. It allowed for a healthy co-existence and that is the maximum Vikas could have hoped for. For all he had today was a gift from God. And his father had taught him early on never to look a gift horse in the mouth. The exact chaste pre-Partition Punjabi phrase escaped him, but it roughly assembled into this. Well, every gift carries with it a curse and Vikas's curse came sooner than later. Sometimes the curse consumed the gift altogether or prevented its enjoyment. In his case it was more the latter.

5.

At the night of the Uto Kulm event, Vikas and Sejal both drank up since there was very little to mingle with in the event. They had hoped to sit with each other on the train ride back to Zurich HB station, but that didn't happen. Sejal did not offer and Vikas did not ask. Yet both yearned for it, but did nothing about it.

Several weeks passed and both did not criss-cross each other in the massive bank headquarters building, till such time as Sejal pinged across a message to Vikas on the Inter-Office Jammer:

"How are things?"

Vikas was hoping for some such chance of taking forward their prior interaction. He would have himself done so if not for Sejal.

"Shall I tell you over coffee?"

"In 20 minutes?"

"Perfect. See you in the lobby."

Sejal wanted to say 2 minutes but wanted to sound less desperate. Desperate for what she did not know. But the potential was there. At the very least she was looking forward to half an hour of unhindered, non-politically correct conversation. In her current state of affairs in the Swiss German heavy department, that was almost like a quickie for a sex starved woman. Not that Sejal had anything to complain about in that department. Prakhar was the most organised data professional in every respect. He had a regimen which few could beat. He was always in control. Never out of step. Prim and proper. The best Mahua had to offer to the world of data analytics or for that matter in the matrimonial market. Predictable and orgasm inducing mostly at regular intervals.

The intervals were never long, such was the precision in everything that Prakhar did. Almost with the robotic routine of many of the algorithms that he managed at the backend for Nestle.

When Sejal saw Vikas alighting from the elevator and making his way towards her, she instinctively ruffled the left side of her jet-black straight hair that was parted in the middle. She had stopped applying *sindoor* ever since she had landed in Zurich. Prakhar never said anything or maybe his algorithm was not programmed to catch such minor bugs.

Vikas restrained extending his hand and Sejal tightly clutched her phone with both hands and pleasantries were exchanged. Vikas led the way to Confiserie Sprungli, only forty seconds away from the main door of Banque Wedderburn Privee. He wanted to make the most of the coffee break that Sejal had stolen away from her workday. This coffee shop had table service unlike the Starbucks of the world, which meant, they could dive into their shop talk straightaway.

"That was a great night," ventured Vikas.

"Really?" responded Sejal and burst out laughing.

"As in, at least I found the only other *Indian* Indian in this whole office."

"Not really. There is a roomful of boys from Chennai and Noida fixing some server issues for the last eight months. You want to meet them?"

Vikas couldn't help laughing his gut out. A genuine laugh after what three years in this place!

"So, what else? You enjoying the bank? It's been what six months now?"

"Yes, its better than sitting at home and fretting. Isn't it?

For some reason many of the responses from Sejal seemed to Vikas as if she knew his situation at home. Couldn't be right? How on earth was she always saying things that he wished Rishika would think up?

He decided to investigate further while their steaming hot cappuccinos arrived with the complimentary Sprungli chocolates. Given Vikas spent so much time there as a shield from the environment within Banque Wedderburn Privee, he was always handed over a few extra chocolates. He handed them over to Sejal, who took one.

Sejal hinted a couple of times at how fortunate she felt to be working, as otherwise Zurich or Pune would have been the same. Now if only Rishika could have gotten that clear in her head. Vikas enquired if the grocery shops he had told her were any good. He was surprised to learn that Sejal's husband had found many others with much cheaper options.

"What about Thums Up in a can? asked Vikas.

"What about it?

"Has your husband found that too in Zurich?

"I don't want to challenge him. He will end up finding that too!" Sejal said with a hint of a smile. Prakhar was the sort who had no requirements beyond the basics. Everything was basic. Ticked all the boxes. So, that meant, Prakhar would rarely think about breaking a sweat about Thums Up as long as the basic rations were met.

Vikas was the exact opposite it seemed to her. His only concern was Thums Up in a can. It also occurred to her that Vikas would never venture to Kernstrasse where Prakhar and perhaps the roomful of Chennai boys landed up bi-monthly to stock up rations. Rations to fire up giant smoking pots of some odourful monstrosity which would choke the Swiss German nostrils at their apartment while cooking and in the office once they opened their tiffins.

And with those sweet nothings, Sejal's time was up. Being a marketing assistant meant she was pretty much at the bottom of the food chain in the department and long absences would be frowned upon. Vikas understood that well and even though he wanted to prolong that coffee, it was better to wait for another leisurely time. Perhaps post office.

They promised to keep in touch and went back to their respective floors.

6.

Sejal's married life was anything but spontaneous. Prakhar never left anything to chance. Whether it was the *dhokla* mix or the condoms or the just in case pill for the accidents, it was all neatly stocked up. Sejal had nothing to worry about. Sejal often wondered if his proficiency on the contraceptive shopping had anything to do with the nocturnal activities during Navratras back in Gujarat. She never asked. She thought asking would somehow expose her own lack of experience during those times and Prakhar would judge her. But judge her for what? That she was a virgin till their wedding night in their native Mahua. But wasn't that a desirable quality? Once she got to know what Prakhar did for a living, she often considered herself as a data stack that Prakhar managed. Someone amenable to predictable information flows and algorithmic triggers of data.

The more her coffee sessions both during the day and post work increased with Vikas, she realised, what a random chap he was. No sense of any predictable data flow. Vikas could be trusted to break into a divergent side dialogue on anything that caught his fancy. Once when she had a fancy haircut at a fairly expensive Zurich saloon, expensive by her Gujju standards anyway, she was surprised by Vikas's reaction.

"*Pehle bhootni lagti thi, ab chudail.*"

"Excuse me?"

"First you looked like a ghostess, now you resemble a witch," translated Vikas with a grin on his right cheek.

Sejal had no option but to raise her hand and strike that grin off Vikas's face. Vikas feigned injury and made a grimace. It was the first quasi-intimate touch between Sejal and Vikas. No one made a fuss of it and went back to the business of downing their double espressos at the La Stanza at Bleicherweg.

The net result of a sum total of one hundred and fifty-three coffees over an eight - or nine-month period in Zurich meant, they were ready to take their friendship to the next level. Which meant taking the party next door to the Le Raymond Bar. The wooden booths inside with the cushioned seats gave a lot of privacy compared to the bare tables and narrow chairs at Confiserie Sprungli.

"*Tu peeti hai?*" was more a statement of surprise rather than a question.

Sejal of course was a pro and had tried everything from vodka to whiskey during her college years in Mahua. Given she was far away from other illicit thrills, this one was deemed in her moral fibre to be of an acceptable variety. Gujarat in spite of the proclaimed prohibition laws was one of the most wet states in India. Gujjus lamented that the prohibition laws only made the cost of drinking higher and did not allow them to cut out the middleman.

"Ya. Sometimes."

And that begun another one hundred and fifty-three meetings over matters stronger than just coffee. With that the potential of their relationship just went up one notch higher.

7.

The trouble with office spouses is, that their marital life does not exist on weekends. Instead, they pine for each other. Pine for the weekend to get over.

Conversations between Vikas and Rishika had ground to a stop. It was not acrimonious, but merely a stony cold co-existence. Trying to stay out of each other's way. Vikas went for long walks along the path of the funicular in Zurichberg. He always thanked his stars for his ability to be here.

Rishika sat around the house doing nothing much, occasionally speaking to her mother on the phone where she uttered bored mono syllabic responses to her mother's myriad questions. Of course, Mrs. Pradhan could sense something was not right and, in her heart, she thought Vikas was to blame for it. Rishika seldom mentioned anything in spite of multiple lines of queries from Mrs. Pradhan. She was still in the old-world mould that once married she must keep her parents insulated from further worries.

During these walks, Vikas often wished he would bump into Sejal. He often wondered what Sejal looked like on weekends, since all their rendezvous occurred within the extended office environment. Always in formals. Though ever since their evening venue had shifted to Le Raymond Bar, there was a lot more informality. What coffee cannot do; martini usually does.

On the other side of Zurich, home to Indian IT migrants, Sejal usually was hosting or attending a lunch between the hours of 12:30 pm and 4pm every Sunday. A lunch with other Infoedge staff who lived in the apartments nearby in Seebach. The menu was always predictable. Booze was not even mentioned. The one time they played Antakshri during lunch and some of the ladies felt an orgasmic release just from that! Sejal was so bored of this stuff that she often wondered what it would be like to spend a weekend with Vikas. Just to converse with him, maybe hold hands for a bit, maybe a hug while meeting and while departing, a few high fives. That much and no more. The tease that Sejal Solanki was, meant that she was clear that she was never going to sexually stray from her marriage. At least that's what she told herself, every time in a high potential situation.

The stuff that gets a tease like Sejal going, is being in a high potential situation. Take the temptation of the high potential situation as high as she could and then leave when it just could head only in one direction. It was not a plotted active data flow like that, but that is exactly how it played out every time she was with Vikas.

On his part Vikas could sense the tension build up. Sometimes from sitting across the table in the wooden booth at the Le Raymond to co-habiting the same side in the guise of watching something on the phone. But the nature of Sejal meant there was no release available, and he never would push it. So, this is how this high potential game of seduction, rejection, elation and ultimate dejection was played out every now and then by Sejal and Vikas.

8.

But one -time Vikas and Sejal did stray. Stray away from Le Raymond that is. The stuffiness and the sameness of the place was getting to them. Stuffiness in terms of the overt formality and sameness in terms of where it was taking the potential of their close personal relationship. Equally, the structure of the place with long tables didn't allow for much physical proximity. So, when one day Vikas suggested they meet at Club Bollywood at Badenerstrasse post work, Sejal jumped at the thought.

But Sejal was Sejal for a reason. She would evaluate every action, every expense, every night out on the touchstone of how she would sell it to Prakhar. Selling it was the key. Not that Prakhar ever enquired, but Sejal was always prepared to douse even the hint of suspicion. Vikas's number was saved as Sameera on her phone!

The thought running through Sejal's mind was whether any of her husband's crowd would likely land up at Club Bollywood. Although she was married to a data analytics dude, her intrinsic ability to process parallel scenarios at breakneck speed mentally was legendary. Minus any of the algorithms or flowcharts. Clearly, she was way smarter than Prakhar could ever imagine. Her need for titillation was more mental than vaginal. Though she had to admit to herself that after a few glasses of whiskey she was equally aroused at both ends. Just the escape from the dour atmosphere of scientific precision at home every few weeks gave her sufficient emotional oxygen to get through the next Sunday lunch!

Club Bollywood tested the limits. The mellow whiskey was abandoned, and martinis were flying all over the bar on an otherwise dull Wednesday evening. Their feet were thumping, though not in unison against some dark 1980s ballad. Not that it mattered what the song was, it was loud enough for them to continuously have to move close to each other to whisper sweet nothings. The sort of nothings which was the sustenance of their relationship. Pure meaningless shit to be honest. Strangely, for both Vikas and Sejal, their respective marital lives lacked this meaningless shit. So meaningful had their marital relationships become that this essential nutrient was being sucked out ruthlessly from their lives. So, they sought this narcotic elsewhere.

After four martinis were working on their facial muscles in terms of drooping faces and loose tongues, old flame secrets were flying thick and fast. Silliness in terms of high-fives and knuckle knocks progressed their need for physical contact. Sejal wished Vikas would make a move. Vikas knew he should not and held back stoically even though every muscle in his body and one in particular was straining.

Book VII

Back to the Beginning (2000–2007)

1. The Dice Rolls on Chestnut Street

When Vikas first met Zainab at the Wah Ji Wah Restaurant on Chestnut Street in Philadelphia, it was the most unlikely site for a business meeting. The business of ensuring that funds in a numbered account in Zurich which Vikas managed had to be given over to her. In cash. No questions asked.

Getting the cash from Zurich to Philadelphia in a suitcase was the most efficient part of Vikas's trip. The same network which seamlessly organised vast swathes of cash from various Indian cities to come in the currency of choice to a bank in Zurich had a trusted network which Vikas could quite easily tap into. Meeting these money mules in Switzerland in unsuspecting places like Luzern and Interlaken was a surreal experience. Each of them ran legitimate cash accretive businesses in Switzerland. But wore their *hawaladar* identities with the same amount of pride. Perhaps with the same amount of pride that scions of royal families in India wore the insignia of their defunct kingdoms on their tweed jackets for ceremonial functions. As if anyone cared.

Wah ji Wah was chosen by Zainab since her current boyfriend Bilal who was a student at Drexel University down the road cleaned tables here to pay for his tuition. It was another matter that Bilal's father who owned the restaurant could have loaned his son the money. But he made him work harder than the staff he employed to drill in the value of rigour and hard work and value for money.

Bilal of course did not resent it and felt it his duty to help his father out. Both in terms of work and attracting new customers. Since Zainab did not love him, she made up for it by spreading a good word about the restaurant. It was not difficult because people from as far away as Lahore and La Guardia alike vouched for the Chicken Chargah whipped up by Bilal's father. The succession plan was to tell Bilal the secret recipe when he had toiled his way up the ranks. The recipe was not in writing and could only be shown and there were many a sleight of hand in the process to lay off the disloyal deserter. Some staff who had thought they had learnt enough and ventured off on their own to try their luck at Chicken Chargah replicas bit the dust soon thereafter. In short, there was no one like the astute senior Burhan Mian both in culinary skills and sleuthing equally.

Burhan Mian adored Zainab because this was the only Muslim girl that Bilal had ever invited over to Wah ji Wah. Not that he minded business from the *pukka goras* or *goriyans*, he harboured a fervent hope that Bilal would marry within the faith, even if that faith was from India. After all, didn't his grandfather originate from Rampur before the 1947 partition – one nation, one people, you get the drift of his thoughts.

So, when Zainab Siddiqui in her sky-blue thigh hugging jeans and the white arm length t-shirt paired with white *hijab* landed up at Wah ji Wah, Burhan Mian greeted her with a surprised *Mashallah Wallekum Salam Zainab Bibi.*

"Salaam Walekum Mian Sahab."

"Zainab Bibi what will you have?"

"Mian Sahab I am expecting a guest."

"Zainab Bibi, you have this booth and let me know what you want, till then have this *sherbet,"* said Burhan Mian while extending a tall copper glass full of rose water flavoured *lassi.* There was indeed no place on planet earth that could conjure those flavours. And all of it was a closely held secret.

Bilal dutifully arrived and cleaned the table off any remnants of the *rogni naan*, which no matter how carefully one chewed left behind some amount of crust. Bilal did not love her. But he loved the fact that he could call her his girlfriend. It gave his otherwise mediocre existence at Drexel University and beyond some colour.

He knew that the degree he was enrolled in was only designed to not let him take over the restaurant and expand it all over America, because that was against Burhan Mian's grand plan. The grand plan of having a ramshackle half worn out restaurant tucked away in one far corner of Philadelphia. The grand plan of waiting for Allah to *baksho* a Michellin star. The grand plan of basically not having a grand plan.

He was resigned to performing all menial tasks in the restaurant and knew most of the staffers secretly and some not so secretly pitied him. So, Zainab was like a breath of fresh air for him to have a normal conversation outside of his cardamom flavoured cage where he was serving a life sentence. Life imprisonment till at least the judge, jury, prosecutor and jailor Mian Sahab was alive. He did not wish him death, just wished himself freedom. Freedom to love. Freedom to live. Freedom to do something of his choice. Freedom to say something over and above Mian Sahab's diktat.

Bilal exchanged some non-consequential pleasantries with Zainab under the scorching gaze of Mian Sahab's watchful right eye. The left eye was always on the *tandoor*. Bilal suspected that Mian Sahab's childhood astigmatism which of course went undetected and untreated in Multan had given him this humungous advantage in his late adulthood. The ability to watch two disparate objects with total focus.

The wiring of his brain had as a result been rejigged where he could process, retain and regurgitate two completely separate conversations at the same time. While cleaning the edge of the table, his fingers brushed against Zainab's. Neither felt any current. There was never any electricity that conducted itself between these two souls and yet there was a depth of comfort.

Just then the heavyset main door of Wah ji Wah restaurant creaked open and in came Vikas. Since the restaurant at that hour had hardly any guests, it did not take him much time to zone in his eyes onto Zainab. Zainab had conjured a mental image of Vikas from their numerous telephonic conversations and he was exactly the way she had imagined him to be. Fair, a hint of a stubble threatening to come out but not just yet, slick oiled hair neatly parted to one side and a smile threatening to spread from ear to ear. All in all, very pleasant. Very *changa munda warga* as Mian Saheb would have said.

Bilal noticed Vikas enter from a corner of the open kitchen that he was scrubbing to death and promptly went back to his work. He was neither jealous nor curious. If Zainab wanted to tell him about this meeting she would, if she did not, then she would not. Fair enough. Either way it did not affect his life.

2.

While trying to cement his place within Bank Wedderburn Privee, Vikas had realised early on that his trump card was to ensure he found out as many of the clients that Magnus managed, contacted them when necessary and quickly assure that the bank was open for business and stable. Stable but secret. He quickly realised that if the other members of the bank got to know the book of clients that Magnus and now, he managed, his presence would soon become superfluous. That his Rajouri Garden-West Punjabi Bagh upbringing would not allow.

He was always overtly sweet, but covertly lived by Magnus' business principles. To start with, he did share details of some less lucrative clients, but ensured that he managed the information flow about large-numbered clients carefully, so that the management team never found out enough to establish direct contact. Vikas was even more successful at this than Magnus. Magnus used the power of his persona and the threat of decamping to a rival bank to maintain secrecy. Vikas just used deception by including irrelevant intermediaries in the chain of ultimate command to the beneficial owners of the accounts under his belt.

After a year he had uncovered almost ninety-five per cent of the numbered accounts sufficiently to establish direct contact with the account holders and explain that he had taken over the book from Vikas over numerous first-class flights to India and back. The last five percent which remained unaccounted for in terms of identification details confounded Vikas no end, because there was just nothing he could uncover in India or Switzerland leading him to believe that perhaps these accounts were not of Indians and may have come in error to Magnus. However, the vast sums standing to their credit worried him, because five per cent of these accounts accounted for nearly fifty per cent of the cash deposits with him. Therefore, it was unlikely to be an error by Magnus. Which could only mean that it was meant to be a deliberate design. A devious design put in place to shield beneficiary and account holder identity. No calls were ever received, nor any communication sought. In these rare cases Vikas's explanation to the management and the actual ground reality actually coincided.

Till one day when a letter from a British Virgin Island based trust company landed up requesting a meeting with Magnus. So, he called back the trust company and spoke to Duncan Bauder and happily agreed to host Duncan for lunch in the executive rooms on the sixth floor of Bank Wedderburn Privee.

So, when Duncan Bauder did arrive for the lunch meeting, Vikas had no inkling that the key to the locked five per cent of the numbered accounts in his care were walking in on their own two feet. Over a three-course lunch of poached salmon, bruschetta and lime cheesecake, which Vikas absolutely abhorred, and Duncan liked immensely, they established a working rapport. Duncan was an old school trustee. He did what he documented and documented what he did. Below his office in Tortolla was a World War II era vault which besides being bomb proof contained secrets which could lay bare many of the world's most influential families.

Aaja Baharon Ki Malika, Mausam Badal Jaye Dil Ka. Once again, this song started humming inside Vikas's mind and threatened to spill out from his lime cheesecake-stained tongue. The last time he could not keep this song inside was on the way back from Moradabad after having first seen Rishika. Thereafter at all his pit stops at state borders, it had become customary for the cops to quiz him, "*Aur mili baharon ki malika?*"

The sight of her tight *salwar* suit clad embellished bum and then her slow motion turning around to face him sprang up in his mind. What a different era that was. An era of innocence. An era untainted by banking. An era where he had so little and yet felt so fulfilled. As opposed to now, when he had so much, and the management was only concerned about the identity of five per cent of the client assets!

Duncan moved himself around the leather cushioned armchair in the executive suite and produced a slip of yellow paper from the inside of his Cavali double breasted jacket. Then he got down to business.

"So, I understand that Magnus is no longer expected to join back on duty?"

"That is right. Very sad indeed."

"Well, mighty irresponsible of him not to have left any documents around or standby instructions."

"I don't think he was expecting such an accident," ventured Vikas.

"Of course not, but if something were to happen to me, I cannot allow jettisoning client assets without a formal structure in place. That is the reason people chose to keep money with banks and not in their dog kennel."

"Dog kennel?"

"It's a turn of phrase. Don't worry about it."

As far as Vikas was concerned. He had helped or participated in retrieving cash from places far worse than dog kennels. In fact, human kennels. He recalled a trip to Shimla to a leading industrialist's house where he saw the man opening the flush tank and taking out wads of currency notes before handing them over to him in his old suitcase.

Duncan moved forward and showed him the slip of yellow paper. It was a copy of an original document, which no doubt rested safely in the vault below his office. It didn't make much sense to Vikas at first glance till the digits in the subject line started doing their dance of fury in his mind. They were the digits which the whole bank by now knew. Or at any rate the people who needed to know. The same people who knew nothing about anything when Magnus was around. So, Duncan was the trustee of the trust which controlled those accounts. For whose benefit the trust was created only Duncan knew and with him the secret would go to the burial grounds in Liverpool where Duncan originally hailed from.

Duncan had of course done a full diligence exercise based on other clients for whom he held trust structures. They had generally said good things about Vikas and his helpful nature in resolving issues. The issues were always few and far in between, so when they arose Vikas was able to use his *jugaadu* nature in general to find a solution. They usually stemmed from sending payments or arranging for more monies to be deposited. Payments often in cash in foreign currency to totally unconnected individuals or entities. Not that it caused Vikas any sweat. His credo was: their money, their decision. He just made transaction fees, service fees on an ad valorem basis and that paid his bills. Actually, that's what paid the bills for the entire banking industry everywhere on planet earth.

It was infinitely easier than making travel bookings for West Punjabi Bagh businessmen, who brought their supply chain procurement knowledge to the ticketing world. So "net-net", as was the saying in West Punjabi Bagh to depict the bottom-line position, private banking was infinitely easier and infinitely more rewarding. What was there to complain.

3.

Finally, it happened at Chestnut Street. Zainab had tagged back with Vikas to his hotel room at the beginning of Chestnut Street. She did not know they would end up in bed, but so ending up was a welcome break from the predictable monotony of her life. A monotony of never-ending depression. A monotony of living without life. A monotony of having ceased to even hope to see Varun again.

Her yearning for Varun had neither ceased nor ebbed in so many years. She just needed Vikas to go up the chain. She fervently believed that Vikas knew more than he let on about the source of funds which he from to time disbursed to her on instructions from someone else.

She had this figured out so far. When they moved suddenly from the wedding party in Amroha to San Francisco on the West Coast, it was no accident. It was not as sudden as her father had made it sound. There were several questions she asked her father time and again but never got any convincing answers. Her mom was another revelation. She turned ever more religious and started speaking in Quranic homilies in response to real world questions. And within four months of arriving in the United States of America, her parents put her into the university halls of residence in San Jose and moved to Cleveland in Ohio. So rather she was told they moved to Cleveland in Ohio.

Zainab spent the first two years of her undergraduate education questioning her entire belief system and forbidding her mind from entertaining questions about the improbability of the answers her father gave her. Her father said he was transferred to a scientific laboratory in the US on behalf of IDPL, but she had chanced upon some documents, which were addressed to her father which contained another name. Further, she was surprised when at the US immigration counter, they were escorted by state agents via a special queue, sans the usual ESTA checks. Her mother, no simpleton by any yardstick, simply put it to a high profile posting.

But Zainab knew better than that. After all, her dad used to live in a Type-III quarter in Virbhadra and used to ride a scooter. From there to be escorted via special channels at the US immigration check post in San Francisco- something was definitely weird. Not impossible but weird. And once the separation from Varun was ingrained in her mind, every aspect of this move became a subject of suspicion and eventual derision in her mind's eye.

And then it was all confirmed. She called Varun from her home number and realised that another family was living there. So, Varun had just disappeared in the ether. She called another of her friends at the IDPL colony and they had left also. And then another. And then yet another. As if there was an annihilation of her entire known ecosystem in Virbhadra. Suddenly she was gone from being the girl from Virbhadra to being a girl with nothing left in Virbhadra. She did not give up. She called up the school. Apparently, there was no Varun Dixit, Sheetal Negi or any of the teachers she knew.

Any other girl would have started questioning herself and her hallucinations, but not so Zainab. She could not figure out what was amiss but was determined to find out more. The one thing Zainab did not have access to, was her passport, so there was no way she could travel back to India. She of course sent letters by post with no illusion that they would be responded to.

The one time she got through to the phone at the IDPL main reception asking for Varun's dad, she was transferred to some new Accounts Officer who did not even know anyone by the name of the senior Mr. Dixit. How? It was almost as if someone had erased every living memory of

Virbhadra. No one even knew that her circle existed. What other way to get the word out to Varun?

She felt so secure with Varun around that her world was collapsing in the sanitised environs of Philadelphia. Did she hurtle from one relationship to another in the search for Varun in every man? Or in the search of a man who she could shape like Varun? Zainab had almost given up hope of ever finding Varun again, not because the world had conspired in ways beyond her comprehension, but because she had started to feel that perhaps Varun hadn't done enough to locate her.

Or had he? And failed in every respect just like her? Impossible. Varun could never fail her. Unless he willed it. How could she forget her sitting on the water tank and wishing Varun would transpire and he did. That too within ten minutes. Because that was the connection they had. Because that was the connection they had built. Because that was the connection they deserved. Because nothing could ever stand in between them. Because she had gone against her mother's explicit instructions and Quranic prescriptions in her relationship with Varun knowing that all would be well in the end. All. And here she felt like a town hoe. Whenever she visited her parents, she could not make eye contact with her father, just as he avoided eye contact with her. Both had something to hide. Both had guilt in their soul. One had sinned against the Quran, the other in defence of the Quran. Or so he thought. Or so he wished to justify his actions.

4.

When Zainab met Vikas, it was his first utterance: "Hi, Miss Zainab Siddiqui?" looking in her direction with eyes that intrigued Zainab. The unaccented and slightly coarse English. Bit uneven on the edges and yet endearing in their familiarity. But familiarity to what? Well for starters, very different from the *desi* American twang that passed off for conversations. Conversations that were doing her head in for the last several years –starting from the time she was bundled into this country.

Vikas got down to business pretty soon once they were settled onto the table chosen by Zainab. Vikas was mesmerised by the beauty of Zainab. The vulnerability that her eyes deflected added to her allure. There were no sharp edges in her voice or in her features. When Zainab spoke, her voice echoed some sort of hidden ache in her heart. The one that resonated immediately with Vikas. Because at core his heart had come unstuck in the last couple of years, held together only by the sporadic coquetry with Sejal.

Vikas had a sincerity of purpose which put the other person at ease immediately. Whether it was Rakesh Pradhan or the border cops or for that matter the senior management of Banque Wedderburn Privee. His sincerity came across as the sort which made the other person want to take a chance on him. And he never failed them.

When Vikas focussed his gaze further onto Zainab, he somehow saw in her eyes the same sort of longing as he was facing in his life. Except, while Vikas sought the love he had lost, Zainab sought some answers over and above the love she had lost.

"I have instructions to hand over some money to you," ventured Vikas.

Since nothing surprised Zainab anymore and she had in the past had strange people turning up at various points with money, papers, passports or other travel documents, she no longer raised an eyebrow.

"Sure," said Zainab.

Vikas took out a plastic folder which had neatly placed brown paper envelopes with about twenty -five thousand United States Dollars and handed it over to Zainab. No signatures needed; no paper trail left. Zainab tucked it into her handbag.

Since the core of their business was over, there was nothing left to further discuss. Except Vikas did not feel like getting up and Zainab for some reason wished he would stay longer. Zainab took the first step.

"Would you like some *masala chai* and something to nibble on?"

"Sure," exclaimed a relieved Vikas and wished there would be no undue hurry to bring their order. He couldn't care less what it would be to nibble on as long as he got to get to know Zainab a little better.

Vikas thought Zainab would enquire about the source of the payment but was surprised when she did not.

Recalling that amazing day in Moradabad when Vikas and Rishika had taken the plunge, Vikas felt a twinge of guilt as he was disrobing Zainab Siddiqui. Zainab had ignited certain flames within him, he seldom knew existed. The melody of Zainab's conversations and the vulnerability of her eyes had formed a soul connection. Yes, he told himself, even the likes of him from West Punjabi Bagh could form soul connections.

So, when Vikas entered her on the plush bed of the Crown Plaza on Chestnut Street, just four miles from where Bilal was cleaning the tables at Wah Ji Wah, it unleashed a tempest of emotions both ways. Not the types that pure testosterone meeting oestrogen does, but one that wiping away years of a tortured soul does. Something just clicked. The curtain fell the minute they were gridlocked in passion.

For the first time in so many years, she forgot Varun for a while. For the first time since his marriage to Rishika, Vikas rediscovered his mojo. Not the mojo that scoring in the bedroom brought in. But the mojo that finding a connect to the soul brought in. Not driven by lust. At least not entirely. A sense of serenity spread across their entire beings.

Zainab was looking for Varun in Vikas. Vikas was looking for the Rishika he thought he had married. Not the Rishika that Zurich had turned her into. Or so he thought that the blame lay at the doors of Zurich.

5.

Zainab and Vikas were a couple in the US. Vikas and Rishika were decoupling faster than US government fines were tumbling Swiss banks in Zurich. The only thing that held Vikas and Rishika together was the ambiguity of the space beyond decoupling. Their relationship had crippled itself largely on account of Rishika's inability to make peace with her life in Zurich.

So, every time that Vikas travelled to the US which was at least six times a year for over 15-20 days at a time, he and Zainab were together. And then Orkut Buyyokoten almost drove a final and decisive wedge between Zainab and Vikas.

Not far away from Zainab's original digs in San Francisco before her move to Philadelphia, Orkut was stealthily launching a social networking site which was connecting people across the globe at a pace never seen before. It was the first time that you could find friends long separated with the click of a button. The more profiles that were created on the website, the more profiles that it attracted. What was first a dorm room rage and then across the Stanford campus spread like wildfire. The universities across the US were early adopters and it suddenly unleashed such a spike in casual dating that condom manufacturers were counting their blessings.

By 2004, Orkut had acquired over 250 million unique users, roughly over sixty per cent of which were females or men who pretended to be females for reasons best known to themselves. It was at this time that Affinity Media launched a law- suit against Orkut and his new employer Google Enterprises for trade secret misappropriation. When Google's General Counsel Celina Brown was discussing the law-suit with Orkut to get to the nub of the code he had written, just one sentence struck her as evocative. When asked by Celina on what inspired him to set up Orkut, the response was: "To re-unite lost lovers."

Celina, the hard-nosed intellectual property lawyer that she was used to the rough and tumble of law- suits flying around across different county courts took note and dropped off a quick mail to her external counsel and moved on to the next matter. If only moving on for lost lovers was that easy. For Celina, Orkut or her external lawyers only had to record dispositions and organise discovery exercises. The lost love was for others to find.

Böök VIII

Bëginning öf thë Bëginning (1992)

1. The Amroha Uprising

That day when Zainab was there to attend the family wedding in Amroha, two things happened. One against her will and the other for her well-being. The trouble is she lost on both counts.

The Ulema of the Saudi funded local mosque took a great liking to Zainab's mannerisms and immediately asked Mr. Siddiqui if his son and Zainab could be betrothed in marriage. In any event Wahabi Islam demanded girls to be married before the age of 15. Zainab was approaching 18 so the hint was that she was past her expiry date.

It did not take Mr. Siddiqui a nano second to mentally dismiss this suggestion and was mentally conjuring a ploy to refuse this indecent proposal. It had less to do with not wanting to be associated with a family of religious fundamentalists in mid-town Uttar Pradesh and more to do with his social contract with Zainab. He had brought up Zainab with a value system where she had the agency of choice to make her own decisions free from any external pressure. Hyderabad, that way was the perfect grounding in such an education, where the Ulemas were kept at a safe distance from one's upbringing. The Ulemas were like television channels in Hyderabad. You could switch them on and switch them off at will. There was enough of a world outside for a Zainab Siddiqui to breathe free. But not so in Amroha.

The reductionist nature of thinking in Amroha was a bit gut wrenching. The Ulemas had locked a large proportion of their followers in an existential battle with the majority community. The dictum was simple. Marry young and reproduce furiously to set up an army to take on the majority community.

The majority community was no better off in Amroha. They had their own Mahants feeding off petty insecurities. Not that it affected the commercial discourse among the two communities. That continued almost in a religious zoog water ball. Inside it all hunky dory. Outside it a total retrograde amnesia of what happened within.

It is this dual living which had preserved peace largely in Amroha for many decades, barring minor skirmishes which were more personal than religious. But Amroha had no permanent escape from the religious bigotry. Unlike Hyderabad, there were neither swanky malls to have a temporal release, nor the BPO industry to earn the cash to burn in the malls. The youth who did not leave Amroha were destined to lead a life looking after small businesses which due to the nature of the ecosystem would never grow beyond a point. And that point had been breached several decades ago. So, the only connection to a greater purpose in life was provided by the religious folks, who made them feel larger than their eight feet by four feet shops or fields of a slightly larger dimension.

But that ought not have confounded Mr. Siddiqui. After all, the Ulema household had every luxury that even houses in Hazratganj Lucknow or Civil Lines Bareilly lusted after. So, in a sense, if any marriage proposal was worth considering in Amroha it would have to be one of the Ulema linked families. Religion was their business and that is the only business that was flourishing.

2.

Since, Mr. Siddiqui had never even brought up the topic with Zainab or her mother, they never knew this background. That is till the curse of Virbhadra befell them. Many of the Hindu colleagues of Mr. Siddiqui warned him about the violent Hindu mobilisation occurring prior to the looming municipal elections in many Hindu majority towns of Uttar

Pradesh and he should take steps to stay within the IDPL compound.

He did that religiously and never shared his insecurities with his family. Till one day when he just couldn't. A junior Muslim employee at IDPL was passing by on a Friday afternoon and they happened to exchange a few words. What Mr. Siddiqui learnt was that he was taking leave for two months. Leave without pay. That too for settling his family of three teenage daughters within the precincts of a large Wahabi mosque in Badaun. They would be safe there. But what was the trigger? Mr. Siddiqui and the junior employee both had lived and tried to come to terms with religious overreach from the lumpen elements of Hinduism. Rather the religious capitalists of Hinduism. Those who capitalised religion to derive profits for reinvestment in the same toxic cycle. The best form of capitalism. Zero capital investment linked to manifold returns. Plus, the added heft in the community. Plus, the halo. Plus ,the recognition of doing something worthwhile, while actually being a vermin of the highest order. They were not delusional, just cold calculated *haramis*.

Several gory tales of crime were shared by the junior employee. They could be the truth. They could be a legend. No one knew. Because no report would ever be filed, and no justice would ever be sought by or dispensed to those harmed. But the fear psychosis travelled far and wide. Exactly as was desired by the religious capitalists.

Was this insecurity new? Wasn't there always an undertone to their religious identity? The undertone which threatened violent change to their faith. The undertone which promised hell if one fell out of line. The line of tolerance which the majority community's religious capitalists could draw at their will. The retribution for any deviant act by a Muslim member anywhere in the world was equally distributed across the fates of every other Muslim. More so in Uttar Pradesh.

Should Mr. Siddiqui take these calls for *palayan* at face value and set up a safehouse in the company of Ulema Sahib in Amroha. Or perhaps go back to Hyderabad? Mr. Siddiqui was a man of solutions. He had always faced his demons within by setting up an escape route. An escape route that would be decisive. He had everything that he needed lined up. Not now, but for years now.

The only thing he could not justify to himself was whether putting his family's safety before his nation would term him a *gaddar*. A *gaddar* with the knowledge and comfort that his family is safe. Or a patriot with his daughter gang raped in the sugarcane fields of Amroha or beyond the walls of the IDPL compound and grinding his heels and his daughter's soul running between courts, police stations and hospitals. All for no justice at the end. The one certainty that Mr. Siddiqui had was that justice would always elude the general masses. No one that he knew had ever got any justice from any institution in independent India.

But why was he thinking up these scenarios? Surely, these are things that happened to other people, and you read and lamented about in the office canteen and got back to work when the cup of tea was over. Perhaps in the times gone by. A virulent right wing Hindu mob of unemployed lumpen youth had shattered that peace in much of Uttar Pradesh. Wastrels who besides the political patronage would have been classified as *goonda* elements and put behind bars, were suddenly the saviours of Hindu *dharam*. They had become the new foot soldiers of a political army propelling the party who had emerged from 2 seats in the Lok Sabha to supporting a minority government in the saddle post the last elections.

Everything would fall into a lazy equilibrium as it always did. Of course, the naysayers would be proven wrong. Mr. Siddiqui had passed through such cyclical motions in the past and had generally been out of harm's way. But that was when Zainab was much smaller. He had done his level best to give her a modern education away from the torchlight of the Ulemas and *madrasas*, never imposed any rituals unless Zainab herself wanted to partake in them. Not to bethrow her in marriage to the Amroha Wahabi family, where he knew she would be safe from the physical issues but deeply mentally unseated. That would be sacrilege. On the contrary to continue living in Uttar Pradesh in these climes would take away every moment of living peace. His god knew how much he had internally gone through all these years.

That's when Mr. Siddiqui pressed the nuclear button.

3.

When Mr. Siddiqui made a day trip to Delhi to the US Embassy, people in office assumed he had gone to further the technology transfer matter. For Mrs. Siddiqui and Zainab, it was just like any other day when Mr. Siddiqui left to go to office. Except it wasn't.

For over seven years, Mr. Siddiqui had made several visits to the Office of the Technology Attache in the US Embassy on Shanti Path in Delhi. The wind dried crunchy orange leaves which outlined the broad boulevards of Shanti Path seemed to be like the shreds of Mr. Siddiqui's life that he was prepared to leave behind.

What had amused Mr. Siddiqui was that the Technology Attache had changed four times in the last seven years, but each one picked up the pieces and stuck to the script. The script that required certain equipment and spare parts to be purchased by IDPL and other research laboratories in India under a framework agreement signed between the two countries. Fairly straightforward.

What was not so straightforward was an implicit understanding between Mr. Siddiqui and the Technology Attache to continuously send across requisitions for spare parts. Nothing wrong there. Except those spare parts never fitted the machinery. Mr. Siddiqui would dutifully refer those to a technical committee and used his executive powers to requisition replacement spares pending the outcome of the technical committee. Mr. Siddiqui suspected that the Technology Attache had similar arrangements with specifically chosen Procurement Officers of other Indian undertakings, but neither was he told nor was it his position to ask.

He also knew that a set percentage of those spares could be his, if he ever asked. He was offered several times, but he never took a penny. Not one penny. However, the Office of the Technology Attache ran a tight ship via a stream of offshore companies where every penny that Mr. Siddiqui turned down was dutifully deposited. He was always assured that this was his for the taking whenever he felt like.

What Mr. Siddiqui had instead negotiated was a placement within the famed Witness Protection Program in the US, where he and his family would be given a new set of identities, a secure place to stay and an ability to begin life afresh in the US. He had been assured over the years, that this could be done within forty- eight hours of his request and how grateful the Office of the Technology Attache was for his constant help in their strategic objectives.

The strategy was two pronged. The Office of the Technology Attache was tasked with ensuring maximum sales of certain obsolete US government owned technology to developing countries. All good, except, the Office never really wanted the technology transfer to be fully self-reliant and complete. As per their deep state mandate, such technology transfer ought always to be work in progress. Since that meant the US government agencies could sell the end products, usually generic life-saving drugs. So, it worked very well indeed. They could earn from their own obsolete technologies and at the same time earn a higher margin from disposing off the end-product at premium rates to the Indian government.

This slick sleight of hand required many many committed followers like Mr. Siddiqui. Each of these were hand-picked by serious brains within the US spy establishment based on an algorithm of multiple factors. Greed alone was never enough to lure a committed Indian worker, it would always have to be based on deep seated insecurities, which they played on.

What amalgam of factors worked to pick up Mr. Siddiqui he would never know, but he always felt being a Muslim in a Hindu majority organization had something to do with this. It of course did not take a genius to figure this one out. But why him? In his heart, Mr. Siddiqui knew that his transfer from the heart of IDPL Hyderabad to the crucible of identity politics in Uttar Pradesh was not just a coincidence or routine transfer as it was made out to be. It was timed quite precisely to coincide with certain other going ons in the state which in one way or other would prick at his armour of security. And so it did. He often marvelled at the precision of the operation that was running behind the scenes and often wondered how many other committed workers were there, which in this organization worked at the behest of the US deep state.

Mr. Siddiqui over the years had developed a habit of frequently taking off his gold rimmed glasses. The sort which was neither stylish nor grand, but a strange sort of effective. Much like his own persona. Neither flamboyant, neither over the board, but just got the job done. For his organization, for his family, for his daughter. And every time he took off his glasses he wiped the lenses with his chequered handkerchief, which Mrs. Siddiqui ironed very carefully every day before he put it in his pocket. Unlike others of his ilk, he never blew his hot breath to moisten the lens. After a couple of wipes, he held it at a distance to make sure every speck of dust had disappeared.

Usually, that was the case always. Except, the specks of dirt that remained in his horizon. The beads of worry. Graphic images of Zainab spread eagled in the sugarcane fields of Muzzafarnagar with maggots crawling out of her ears and vultures feasting on her naked body. The mob does not discern between class, qualification or position. The mob is hard wired to inflict damage, acquire power and disenfranchise the other. Here he was the other and perilously so. He would not have thought twice if it was just him. But having heard about what was happening in nearby towns by the radical trident wielding Hindu mobilisation, he could not rest in peace knowing that Zainab would be left to her own devices. Even the IDPL colony did not feel safe anymore.

He could of course seek a transfer to Hyderabad, but the way the government processes ran, it would be several years before a decision would be taken. And given the macro dynamics at play within IDPL, he had no doubt that he had only one exit. Classic chess move. He would be safe and so would be his small kingdom, but there was just one way.

Since he never received any monies for this through the last seven years, he never considered it corruption and justified it to himself and his Allah. He kept telling himself that he would never have to enter the golden cage promised by the

US Federal Witness Protection Program and it was only a disaster day travel pass.

There were moments when he had come close to exercising it, but held back, since this was the *brahmastra*. It could only be used once. And once used, it would cause all round destruction. And so, it did.

4.

Zainab and Vikas were an all-out item in Philadelphia. After a while, Zainab felt such a level of comfort with Vikas that she had forgotten the entire purpose of her getting close to Vikas was to find out the full story of her sudden removal to the US. Not that Vikas knew even an iota of it. He was just a banker who was in charge of executing payment instructions at Banque Wedderburn Privee. And in true Swiss tradition, no questions asked, no answers given. But every instruction was executed on priority efficiently.

If the instruction required wiring monies to certain accounts, he did it. If the instructions were to physically hand over wads of bank notes wherever needed, he did it with equal panache. He had no clue why he received calls from certain tax havens from time to time to deliver bank notes of a certain order to Zainab. But he was not complaining.

Zainab was his second lease of life after all. She was the last embodiment of any semblance of life that he had hoped that he and Rishika would lead after his new -found prominence in life. Whereas, he had hoped that being a senior private banker based in Zurich at Banque Wedderburn Privee would have made Rishika proud of him and improve their relationship, that never happened. The Moradabadi damsel that he had so loved had ceased to exist in the Swiss Alps. What remained was just a distant memory of happier times. Even his West Punjabi Bagh romance just after his marriage to Rishika was of more consequence than the last five years in Zurich.

Vikas knew he could not go back to India, for here he felt content within Banque Wedderburn Privee and thanked his stars a couple of times a day for the enormity of the opportunity that had landed on his lap. From being a cash mule for Magnus Montgomery, he had in effect become in the last five years one of the largest revenue earners for Banque Wedderburn Privee and a sought- after private banker in the incestuous Swiss market.

And his value was essentially dealing with banking arrangements outside of India. A butterfly could not go back into a cocoon and that was his sad state. It was wonderful being a butterfly, from being a worm of the banking universe in the grand scheme of things. Except his mate had detached her wagon from his train. Vikas had loved every moment from the first day he had walked in through the gold embossed miniature vault type doors of Banque Wedderburn Privee. His rustic charm had won over the receptionist, who over the years had turned into his sartorial consultant. From wearing dark shirts and shiny ties with black suits reminiscent of *baraats* on GT Road on the periphery of Delhi and Karnal, he had graduated to the more sombre Swiss style of dressing. Understated, yet classy. It was not his first preference but made him more effective both inside the bank and outside of it. Senior management warmed up to him slowly, from wanting him out to not wanting to let him out of sight. They were very impressed by the way he adapted and managed to rescue a certain loss of business to the bank. So, he was now one of the inner circle. Not by choice, but by happenings around. Not that he complained but had the same wide-eyed wonder every time he replayed the sequence of events in his mind.

At heart very little had changed. From driving a second hand Maruti 1000 with brass pots and pans, he roamed around Zurich in a Range Rover with a Tute leather satchel. He had found it so uncomfortable to carry that around initially. He had always preferred a West Punjabi Bagh manufactured backpack, but that just was not par for the course for Swiss private bankers. Since change was his only constant, this too was not beyond him. The receptionist had made him a *banda* as his friends in West Punjabi Bagh would have said. *Banda bana diya launde ko.*

All in all, Vikas had burst onto the private banking scene minus any background, training or pedigree and had managed to hold his own. His only wish was to reclaim Rishika from the depths she had plunged during this time. She was still pretty, but the sort of sexless prettiness which was almost crying for redemption. What redemption god alone knew. Vikas at home was always in a fragile state, always prepared for some implosion.

Except it was never the violent cathartic explosion of emotions he so wished that whatever she was undergoing would come out of her. It was the slow, corroding, cold, dispassionate soul crushing sort of indifference that had crept into Rishika. All it seemed to matter to her was to climb up to the open terrace of her *mohalla* in Moradabad and glance at will at the far-reaching suburban ugliness of architectural monstrosities. Actually, non-architectural monstrosities. The profession of architecture had never taken off in Moradabad because everyone and her grandmother had grand ideas about designing buildings. Since town planning regulations only meant a paan-stained receipt from the local municipal corporation to register the house for property taxes, no one ever cared about how the houses looked. Let it not be mistaken that the houses were ugly at the start. The fresh coat of white, green, blue or pink paint on the exterior usually lasted the first monsoon. But not long thereafter. Much like the union of Rishika and Vikas. It had a spark. It lasted a few monsoons. But the land of Zurich which never knew monsoons eroded it to such an extent that Vikas could not recognise the edifice that the time has left behind.

5.

The precise point when Zainab crossed over from using Vikas to find Varun, to using Vikas to find her own self back she did not know. Now all she pined for were Vikas's trips to Philadelphia, duly extended by misusing corporate privileges and shacking up in his hotel room or her living quarters. Just putting her head on Vikas's shoulder and looking out of the thirtieth floor of the executive suite of the Crown Plaza onto Chestnut Street made her reminisce the water tank days in Virbhadra.

Strangely looking into the expanse of architectural uniformity that the urban landscape of Philadelphia town offered a hope of some order in her heretofore tempestuous life of the last few years. She never felt any connection with Bilal, but just had him hanging around. Not that Bilal did not know. He had his own reasons to escape from his father's diktats, which were murdering whatever little was left of his self-esteem.

What Bilal did not know was that Zainab's prolonged periods of disappearance from the university coincided neatly with the days recorded on Vikas's expense reports back home in Banque Wedderburn Privee in Zurich. Vikas ostensibly stayed on in Philadelphia to prospect for fresh clients, but he never did. The bank never asked any questions. They could not. He was not Magnus, but he was all the bank had to protect that line of business. He was the last man standing between Mark Scharer being dismissed from an inglorious control failure in managing Magnus. Mark in the winter of his career could not afford being dismissed and thus started yet another egregious episode of creating another Magnus-like monster.

6.

When Vikas got down at the Zurich HB station after the ten-hour flight from Philadelphia, he strolled alongside the Limmat thinking about his life. He held onto the rail which separated Old Town and the glitzy new town of Zurich. It would have been poetic if the rail signified the departure from his old life and the new life that he was holding onto, but it was the Limmat which was most poignant in its bearing.

The Limmat in many ways signified to Vikas how quickly the sands had shifted. So clearly, yet so definitively and the space he just cast his eye on had flown away, never to return again. He wished he could have a normal life with Rishika. In spite of all his transgressions with Zainab, she was again like the Limmat – here now and gone again. He could not for his life become the apparition of whoever Varun Dixit was. His mind grated every time Zainab mentioned Varun. Why was it that in the end he, Vikas was the one without someone who loved him to the other side of the planet earth and back. He did not feel as envious of Varun as he felt pity on himself. He had tried everything. This journey had not been easy and yet he felt a sense of personal abandonment at home.

He did not feel like taking the Seilbah Riglibick up to his posh residence on Zurichberg hill. As posh as his new -found wealth would allow. A wealth he would have happily traded back to regain whatever of left of his marriage to Rishika. He had no illusion about a future and family with Zainab. From wanting just, a normal affordable life to landing in the lap of unimaginable riches, only to be defeated.

Defeated by Rishika. Nothing that he had garnered made for pleasant consumption now. The toxic cocktail was threatening to cut the main oxygen of his life. His carefree nature. When would he next sing *Aaja Baharon ki Malika* which so regaled state border police forces in north India?

When would he next break into a smile which spread from ear to ear without wrinkling up near the sides of his eyes? When would his work become fun again? The same rush he felt when he first landed at Zurich Flughaven from Delhi lock, stock and wife in tow. How wide his eyes opened when the clean environs of the Zurich airport greeted him? How wide his eyes opened when he saw the employment contract at Banque Wedderburn Privee for the first time? Now he just seemed to collect the salary with no joy whatsoever. His many accomplishments which kept the senior management very happy were like water off a duck's back. This could not go on for long. Something had to give. And then it did.

7.

Orkut single handedly managed to do what no US government double agent could have done. It helped infiltrate the US Government Witness Protection Program. Varun zeroed in on Zainab via Orkut. Literally. The volley of abuse peppered with liberal doses of Deccani Hyderabadi ones which left Zainab's tongue like darts confused the messaging system on Orkut enough for it to stall a few times. Not before Varun had left a message reading: PA 19104.

Zainab's heart pounded. That was also the post code for Bilal's restaurant. Was that rascal Varun on Chestnut Street all this while? Was he lost to the world only to be found on Chestnut Street while she became the biggest town hoe that Philadelphia town had ever seen? Why oh why was this happening? Just when she had started to find a rhythm with Vikas that Varun had appeared literally from the dead?

She was at the same time juggling three relationships. The fake one with Bilal. With full knowledge and acquiescence of Bilal. The sexual one with Vikas, which was threatening to spill over onto something serious. At least that is what she feared. She could not put into it what Vikas was prepared to put in and Vikas knew it. And now the real one, the one that had changed her as a person. The one that had shaped her as a person. The one that had not left her more than five years after she had left India. The one she heaped much of the blame for her current state on, in spite of it never having been in the picture for the last so many years.

When these many emotions churn in one's mind, the skull is not enough to contain them. The emotions holler down the throat and move up and down the oesophagus. One churn more and the reflux would be impossible to contain. Zainab felt sick at her core, while typing: 3200 Chestnut Street – Come there.

Varun wrote: Leaving now.

Zainab shut her computer and clanged shut her hostel door at the halls of residence and left without her cap or scarf. Just her white overcoat which had been her faithful companion since her West Coast days. More faithful than Varun. By the time she climbed down the iron wrought staircase of her halls of residence, a semblance of disbelief had started to permeate her thoughts. Disbelief about the fact that she was more enraged than amorous. Disbelief that she was more content at having found Varun in a test score sort of relief than the actual joy of having found lost love. It was almost the relief at the end of a long winding project that refused to cease.

She did not feel the illicit thrill that Virbhadra always brought to her body before meeting Varun. The thrill that coagulated at the centre of her bosom and every then and now travelled south. Sometimes very south. The thrill which only subsided when she and Varun were locked together in coital harmony. That was the only feeling that she ever longed for while in Virbhadra.

Maybe the longing and the endless wait and the ever-mounting anxiety had numbed the erogenous zones of Zainab's body. The same zones which got activated so effortlessly in Virbhadra. But sadly no longer. Maybe they would recover. Just not yet. Not that she was thinking about this. Her mind was just blanking out. Actually, not blanking out, but blacking out. The tsunami of emotions had flooded her brain in a way that she could not even feel the Philadelphia winter which minus her scarf was chilling her spine while walking the two blocks to Joe's Coffee. The last thought while fixing up Joe's Coffee as the meeting place with Varun was the need to be as far away from Wah Ji Wah as possible. She could not bear to put Bilal through more. Howsoever fake, she knew her relationship with Vikas had taken a toll on Bilal's confidence levels which any way was rock bottom thanks to his tyrant dad.

She had made a mental note to have a talk with Bilal and disengage formally. So that he could at least announce that he had dumped her, or some find some such redemption. At least someone in their complex world could find some solace. She was under no illusion that meeting Varun would bring any sort of solace. It would possibly complicate everything furthermore.

True that Varun had initiated contact on Orkut. Was it too late? Was the launch of Orkut the only reason why Varun found her? What if Orkut never launched? Why was she thinking these thoughts? Shouldn't she be happy that finally Varun and Zainab were to unite? In any case what was Varun's fault in the whole game? Game indeed.

8.

"Behen ke laude kahan tha tu? Harami kahan muh kala kar raha tha," the words came out involuntarily as Zainab grasped Varun close to her chest and whispered into his ears.

"You are the one who left without any ceremony."

"I thought you would find me from the dead."

"So, isn't that what I have done?"

Tears started rolling down Zainab's cheeks and Varun's university sweatshirt was soaked on one shoulder. This catharsis was overdue five years. The beauty of it was the decibel levels. All of this was happening with such decorum that not one idler in the coffee shop took notice. Nor did the baristas or the owner of the family run coffee shop on Chestnut Street. No one could even guess the momentous occasion that was taking place within the precincts of a Chestnut Street coffee shop. It was almost a re-run of the scenes from the top of the Virbhadra water tank minus the sexual element. This was pure raw human emotion at its core. Emotion which was too ripe to contain within any longer.

Varun had rimless glasses now which made his fair face with his wavy hair and smallish forehead look rather mature for his years. He always had an impish grin which endeared him to all and Zainab especially, which had disappeared somewhere. Varun had become all brawn and very little of the smalltown goodness was exuding from him. Somewhere before Zainab stood a branded version of her *desi* boyfriend. The contours of him felt the same way, but a hardness had permeated his face. As if a chisel had chipped off the excess *desi ghee wala* chubbiness and given an angular appearance. His Adam's apple was prominent and did not feel very edible. She wondered what was going through Varun's mind right now. How does one even begin to compress five years of absence? An absence which had bored acidic wells in their hearts.

Twenty minutes from their arrival and they were still in an embrace. The tears had dried, but neither Varun nor Zainab were letting go of each other. Neither found it odd. No one else bothered. Soon it became apparent to both Varun and Zainab that the coffee shop would shut at its appointed hour of 8 pm and they would have to leave. All of the chairs had been upturned onto the coffee tables and the owners were making the final checks on the equipment. As Varun and Zainab finally broke their embrace and sauntered out into the dark Philadelphia winter, Zainab sat down on the sidewalk. She just could not walk a nanometre. It was almost as if every ounce of energy had departed her body. She felt dehydrated but could not emote it. Varun also hunkered down on the sidewalk. The impracticality of the situation was lost on both.

Varun in his sweatshirt, drenched on the right shoulder. Zainab in her unbuttoned overcoat and flimsy t-shirt below. Both were howling their insides and yet holding onto each other in an awkward pose on the Chestnut Street sidewalk. There were not many people walking at that hour. But then who was bothered. Neither Varun nor Zainab could master the courage or energy needed to put a structure to their being at the moment. To try and piece together their last five years in wilderness. In exile from each other. In exile from their true feelings for each other. Another couple of hours went by when finally, the sub - zero temperature got to their bones. Zainab could hardly move, and Varun's teeth started clattering against each other. Finally, the honeymoon was over. Finally, the environment had weaned them from the idyllic setting of just letting their emotions flow.

Varun tenderly got up and placed his arms around Zainab's shoulders and pushed her close to his chest and they started limping towards Varun's apartment. It was a good fifteen - minute walk and by now Varun was sure that they would both die of frost bite. An apt ending to an epic love story indeed. Death without any material words having been exchanged. Death without any of the great secrets having been spilt. When they climbed the two flights of stairs onto Varun's studio apartment on Walnut Street, he could have sworn that professional mountain climbers would not have been so fatigued.

9.

In the meanwhile, Varun and Zainab were not fucking like rabbits. In fact, they were not fucking at all. Quite surprising since every relationship that Zainab had entered into before was centred around sex and hanging out in noisy university joints. There was never any soul touching conversation. In fact, Zainab had earnestly believed that her soul had been incinerated. Till Vikas walked into her life. And now Varun.

With Varun, she was able to piece together the last several lost years of her life. Her abrupt uprooting from Virbhadra. The proposal from Amroha. The razing of the Akbari Masjid near Gajraula. The sudden turning to religious text for Mrs. Siddiqui. The turning in of her father. The strange people around them. The chaperone for her grandmother's funeral in Muzzafarnagar. The spelling error in her passport, which percolated to her university records. The mysterious addition of a prefix Bibi to her name. From being Zainab Siddiqui in Virbhadra she had become Bibi Aasna. Not that she ever had a moment of peace to investigate any of these loose ends. She was all too focussed on finding the Varun Dixit.

But now that she had found him and finally the tears had dried, surprisingly but in fact so had everything else. For a while after the jigsaw had fit together and nothing else remained to be exchanged, it stopped precisely there. Varun and Zainab were both surprised. They had imagined their eventual union in a very different way. But this transactional way of exchange of information and emotion and then a dead end confounded them both. Perhaps this is what closure meant. No further rights to anything and no further obligations of anything. Just total and complete erasure of each other going forward. It was not effortless. All the tears and debilitating conversations to piece together the last several years was the effort. But once done, it was done. Done for good.

The emotional switch off was so sudden and so pronounced. Even a ceiling fan once switched off meanders to a stop slowly, but in Varun and Zainab's case, it was almost as if the ceiling fan stopped dead in its tracks. There was no further motion. So, when Varun dropped off Zainab near her apartment, they exchanged a quick lifeless hug. Almost as if two emotional corpses were embracing and disengaging. What had happened was that they had moved on from the water tank in Virbhadra and unlike films all reunions howsoever tearful were not meant to be. This was one of them.

Book IX

Meanwhile In the World (1992 onwards)

1. Ayodhya Se Aage

If the Babri Masjid demolition left the towns of Amroha and Virbhadra untouched from the scorched earth tactics of ascendant Hindu nationalist groups, it was not for long.

Prakash Chand Trivedi, who was a classmate of Rishika in Moradabad had a realisation quite soon after graduating from their mofussil college with a degree but no employable skills. The realisation was that the only campus placement seemed to be from the local VHP *shakha*. It provided some income and an enormous veneer of local respectability. Far more than any job as a bookkeeper anywhere in the Rampur-Moradabad belt could have brought in. But the job was obviously more challenging than being a bean counter.

When Prakash was called for his orientation at the VHP *pramukh's* Agarwal *gali* residence, he was in no doubt that quasi-criminal activity would be involved in his day-to-day job.

"Darne ki koi zaroorat nahin. Sarkar hamari, manzil hamari." This was what was repeated to them time and again by various esteemed faculty members who outlined the multifarious incidents of eve-teasing by Muslim youth and how breaking down Muslim places of worship in and around their jurisdictional limits would magically wean away Muslim youth from such immoral activities.

And so, the work began. From destroying small round the corner green flag establishments, to very tiny mosques to defacing *kabrastans* to throwing pig meat in front of mosques, it was all part of a gruelling day's work. It involved the thrill of a local sub-inspector's job without any of constraints of the procedures and protocols. They were after all Hindu warriors, not petty land-grabbers. That is what he would graduate into after many years of dutifully following instructions of doing Ram Lulla's bidding with a *trishul*. Very soon, there would be more unemployable youth and far fewer Muslim places of birth, death, procreation and recreation left in Moradabad. What then? That was the promotional time when the local VHP pramkukh would go to the headquarters and get a slightly larger ambit to grab land. And this is how the real estate business prospered in some of the most deprived towns of Uttar Pradesh.

Prakash and Rishika did not really know each other, yet his actions on the world at large had the most profound impact on her life. But for the likes of Prakash and their frolics at playing Monopoly with Muslim real estate zones, Mr. Siddiqui would never have fled Virbhadra. Given the polarisation in Western UP, Mr. Siddiqui did not consider the Amroha mosque fuelled by Saudi Wahabi dinars as a sanctuary. He instead uprooted his family entirely and went under the Witness Protection Program in the US in lieu of certain services rendered. No trace left. As if the family had vanished into thin air. And it did.

Just when Rishika was finally emerging from her shell in Zurich. Finally, when she could see the damage that her behaviour had inflicted on their marriage and on Vikas, he had checked out. Checked out mentally. No proof was required, because the Vikas in his swanky clothes had become a shadow of his former self.

He neither engaged nor got enraged. He spent so much time out of the house that she never even realised when he was inside or outside. Any communication was answered with a cool measured response. As if always on the tenterhooks to prevent an outburst. Outburst was all that Vikas had become accustomed to. For everything that Zurich got him professionally, it took away far more personally. He had never thought he would become involved with Zainab like a man gets involved with a narcotic substance. He does not love it but cannot do without it. He would take enormous risks to get it and end up sacrificing everything.

Not that Vikas ever hurt Rishika any other way than just withdrawing himself totally and absolutely. For long it never mattered to Rishika and when it did Vikas was just not there.

2.

No doubt Wahabism imported from Saudi Arabia was putting up a tough fight in the battle for prime real estate in Western Uttar Pradesh. The agents of Wahabism were in general upper middle class property sharks who could easily slip in and out of the Koran. And somehow the apparatus for gathering such sharks in large numbers was progressing rather well.

The likes of Prakash Chand Trivedi were no match for the organizational and business skills of Maulana Saheb. The way they blended religion with property left a lot of eager students awestruck. In the end no one was wiser whether they had consummated a property transaction or a religious one. However, the only truth was that they had been consummated. Penetrated headlong by Wahabism and sentenced to serve in *Allah*'s hall of dishonour via express deviations of the Koran that Wahabism imposed for life.

The beauty of the Wahabi Islam brand spreading across UP was that it was a complete multi-modal marketing model.

There was just no local reporting, unlike the VHP. Every Maulana anywhere was the captain of his ship and the master of his destiny. They communicated directly with some Ullemas in Saudi Arabia. Also, the deliverables were to garner as much land and make believers of as many Muslims as possible. That was not difficult when their madrasas flushed with funds hosted lavish meals every now and then to keep the army of foot soldiers happy. The army which could be assembled at a moment's notice if any danger from the local VHP hudlums lurked nearby. Thus, continued this elaborate yet simple property acquisition and protection program.

Where Mr. Siddiqui could not get confidence from this setup enough to bethroe Zainab in marriage to the Junior Maulana in Amroha at the prime age of eighteen was the enemy within. It was in no doubt that being betrothed to the Maulana household gave a large degree of protection that he Mr. Siddiqui on his own could never afford. But to what sort of life? Zainab would have been reduced to a side furniture in that household and perhaps made to regress in her mindset. If Mr. Siddiqui had never embarked on a modern education for himself or his daughter this would have been too good an opportunity to pass up, but no more. Not that Mr. Siddiqui regretted for a moment putting his only daughter through the best liberal education that he could afford.

So, Mr. Siddiqui sold his soul to the satan. At least that is what the Koran would have classified his action as such. Only post his demise would Zainab ever know, if at all, the conundrum in his mind. The image of his daughter spread eagled and hung from a mango tree in Western UP post a brutal gang rape was too powerful to ignore. Equally, the intellectual gang rape that would occur in the Wahabi household in Amroha was again debilitating. Of course, the Koran would have prescribed a fearless path to discover the truth. Except, Mr. Siddiqui in his frame of mind would have taken upon himself any amount of risk but could not wilfully put any upon Zainab.

By the time the family under the aegis of the Witness Protection Program had landed in the US, Mr. Siddiqui and Mrs. Siddiqui alike were so glad to have escaped what had seemed like certain life changing violence, that they totally abdicated any further upbringing responsibilities to the US state system. Not voluntarily of course. They thought not to taking Zainab into confidence would prevent her from having a negative image of her father's decision. But clearly the emotional abandonment Zainab felt was beyond her parents' wildest imagination. In retrospect perhaps they should have told her. They underestimated her ability to understand. Her ability to cope. Her ability to adapt. Wasn't she after all doing all of that? That too without any of the background or the full picture.

So, when they left Zainab at the halls of residence of the San Jose State University to commence her undergraduate studies under the assumed name of Bibi Aasna, they never thought that they had created a schism between them that only a Varun Dixit could have cured. The Varun Dixit who appeared a full five years later, from the Orkut revolution sweeping across the United States of America.

While in Cleveland Ohio, Mr. Siddiqui did get news of several families that he knew being forced to flee their homes in UP, to either safe havens like Amroha, Deoband, Saharanpur or to places outside India or down South. Those who were not so lucky faced unimaginable cruelty, violence and life altering scars everywhere from psyche to genitals.

Böök X

Back tö thë Middlë (2007 önwards)

1. Ebbing Tides Atop Zurichberg

Fatigue. A single word that was signifying Vikas's existence in Zurich. From his perch at Zurichberg, the small balcony overlooked the entire valley comprising the Old Town, the financial district, the cathedral and the river that dissected the city into the old and new towns. When he had first taken this house in the fancy district that housed fat cat bankers, all he had wanted to do on this balcony was to share a cup of tea with Rishika. But such was the turn of fate that she always found something to do when he was sipping a cup of staid tea on the balcony.

For Vikas, now his house was an extension of the departure lounge at the Zurich airport. Where he stayed only for as long was necessary to catch the next flight out to the US. It was helpful that no one in office ever questioned his trips or queried his expenses. The good part about Swiss private banking was that they never got wiser from mistakes. They only found yet another way to make the same mistake. So, what Magnus had started purely for client confidentiality,

Vikas continued on the pretext of staying further and further away from Rishika.

His joy was totally scorched from within. Almost as if the embers of a burning heart had ebbed and the ashes were flying in the wind. The same wind, which he so cherished walking to the Selfbahn from his Zurichberg house had turned into a lifeless breeze. The sort that morgues and mortuaries possibly had, every time a door opened. A breeze which had emulsified souls trying for one final escape from the trajectory of life. Complete *nirvana*.

The plan was not working. There was no plan. Here he was the youngest Managing Director of an establishment Swiss private bank. His book was the talk of the town. A worthy successor to Magnus had been found. The shop had been saved. Martin was relieved. But what the revenue factory within Banque Wedderburn Privee did not even dream of was that their star banker was imploding within. What the ski slopes did to Magnus, Rishika was doing worse to Vikas. Zainab's soothing balm was like life support for this man, but with Varun back on the scene how long would it last?

Not that Vikas was hoping for anything more from Zainab than the bond he shared. Frankly the sex was purely incidental from being primary in their relationship. Just being able to talk to one another in his *desi* lingo and being understood phrase for phrase outside the Swiss cut and dried industrial precision within the bank was hugely palliative for Vikas. That was it. That was all that he now hoped Rishika would someday recover from her pall and gloom and eternal melancholy. It was not to be.

However hard Rishika tried to bring a semblance of normality to her life, she found yet another issue to quibble with herself and the world around. It could be something simple as the credit card not working at some train station or the quality of Indian groceries that she bought from Tamilian shops on the far end of Talstrasse. Each and every small impediment set her back by years. Not a medical recovery, because there was just nothing wrong medically. Vikas had confirmed it with multiple and expensive shrinks who had spent the better part of their lives on the Swiss Alps from the earnings of disgruntled wives of Swiss bankers. Not really, but not too far from the truth either. Starting from one trip to Moradabad in their first year in Zurich to about six trips a year by the mid-term and now none at all. Her parents sensed something amiss each time they saw Rishika and tried to talk to her, but it did not help.

The unfortunate bit was that even if Vikas picked up the pieces in West Punjabi Bagh now and brought Rishika back there, it would perhaps be a replication of Zurich with none of the gains, if any of Swiss private banking.

Rishika just could not make sense of what was happening to her. She wanted to be desperately happy. She could see the strain that Vikas was under. Vikas had not once raised his voice. If anything, his decibels just went south, and he was just content to not let any utterance of his lead to an emotional conflagration. But her loneliness was corroding her from within and her sense of uselessness in Zurich was debilitating. Rather than enjoy the perks of what came with Vikas's sterling growth within Banque Wedderburn Privee, her own sense of failure cast a shadow on their joint existence. Actually, a shadow was an understatement. It was actually a *suryagrahan* – a total obliteration of light in their lives.

When Mrs. Pradhan had suggested a child would be the panacea to their troubled marriage, Rishika just could not fathom taking on more responsibility. She did not discuss it with Vikas and there was hardly any action under the sheets that could miraculously lead to the arrival of a baby. All for the good. Good of the new-born that is.

Böök XI

Vikas & Zainab: Thë Cröwn Prince and Princëss öf Zurich: Nöw–2018

1.

Vikas and Zainab were sitting in the family compartment of the Swissrail train from Lugano to Zurich. Not by choice, rather by circumstance. Their co-passengers had pesky little boys, aged seven and four. Both monsters of children, who could only be engaged on the slides and other soft play areas in that compartment. The co-passengers were Vikas's colleagues from Banque Wedderburn Privee, who they ran into at the Lugano train station. After an exhilarating pheromone filled weekend, the last thing they wanted was to chat inane nothings on what was a beautiful train ride back.

Thankfully, the boys kept the parents busy, and they had very little to converse on the six-hour train journey back to homebase. However, being in the family car on the train, meant any public display of affection was to be kept at a minimum or preferably at level zero. That was anyway never an issue with Vikas and Zainab. The only closeness was driven by the need to plug in the two end points of the solitary shared earphones to listen to cheap foot tapping Bollywood numbers. The love of that one thing glued Vikas to Zainab and vice-versa quite literally.

In the last fifteen odd years of togetherness, they had taken countless train journeys across Europe. Their clothes changed as did the style of their luggage, but one thing that remained deathly constant was the shared earphone. Many a quaint European meadow in the middle of their road trips or walkathons bear scars of Vikas and Zainab tearing out their earphones and letting loose their ammunition of Bollywood songs as they sat back or sometimes even broke into a jig.

More than any public display of affection, if by any fortuitous circumstance those tunes were heard by the family centric train compartment, the outcomes could be entirely unpredictable. Once at a Bollywood party which was organised every year by Shivani Thakkar from London at the Zurich Museum costing two hundred and fifty Swiss francs per entrant, Vikas was beyond himself seeing fine Swiss German ladies in hip hugging dresses gyrating to *Jeth ki dopahri mein paon jale.* Some of their moves would have put item number dancers in India out of business. He did not want a repeat of that, if for nothing else, but to keep peace with his office colleague. Not that he cared much for office politics or collegiateness - his book of business having assured him permanent and total immunity from these petty pursuits, but yet he wanted to keep a safe distance from any idle chatter.

The second coming is often more profound and considered and so was the case of Vikas and Zainab. If it was not Bollywood, there would have been something else to glue their mental and emotional synergy. Too often relationship columns quoted "getting each other" as a relationship glue, but very few actually got it right. And here Vikas and Zainab had not just cracked the secret sauce – they had hit a home run. It was a pity it was a second chance, because it meant they had a fewer set of years to be with each other. But again, they contemplated that were it the first time around, they may not have valued each other as much. It is only out of profound loss did they actually start valuing profound connectedness to each other. The last fifteen years, they had rebuilt themselves with each other as building blocks to erase the sense of loss. But for each other, they would have been lost to the world. Present in physical form, but totally emotionally absent. That is where their respective past relationships had left them –not wholly out of conscious choice but nonetheless the outcome was exactly as stated.

2.

When Zainab sashayed into the Zurich Museum in her designer *lehenga choli* with Vikas in his tuxedo, a couple of Indian women sniggered. Perhaps about her status with Vikas. But it did not matter to them. It actually never did.

Both had suffered long and hard. One in search and the other in waiting. What mattered was to make good of the present and make up for the past. And make up they did. Vikas and Zainab danced till the early hours of the morning. They would drink and dance till such time as the sleepy staff of the Zurich Museum would plead with the event organisers to vacate the venue. To give them just enough time to clear up the big fat Bollywood party mess to welcome the next troop of art connoisseurs.

What amazed the staff of the Zurich Museum was that year after year the *desi* guests or for that matter their non-*desi* invitees at the Shivani Thakkar Bollywood Ball had never once expressed any curiosity about the priceless artifacts on display in the sanctum sanctorum of the museum. Not once in the last ten years. Clearly this ball attracted some very focused individuals, who knew exactly what they were there for and never deviated from that path. Vikas and Zainab personified that class of people. They had never once in the last many years of being together in Zurich even as much ventured into admiring the world-renowned artifacts.

Once Vikas had to accompany some guests from Banque Wedderburn Privee for a private tour of the collection. When he had returned to his Zurichberg perch, he had a raging headache, which only a shot glass of *desi tharra* bootlegged all the way from West Punjabi Bagh and duly declared at Zurich Customs as cough medicine could cure.

After leaving the Zurich Museum, they would in their ridiculous attire take Tram Number 8 to the Zurich Airport. That was the only place which served any form or shape of food at the unearthly hour of four thirty in the morning. The best thing about anyone watching Vikas and Zainab at a distance gulping food down their throats at a food court inside the Zurich Airport premises was the total obliviousness to any public scrutiny.

They would be silly, they would be serious, they would yell, they would laugh. All for themselves, with not a care in hell as to what the people around thought. They did not care two hoots. And that was the basis of their relationship. They did not care two or four or however many hoots society demanded, about the Indian community in Zurich or for that matter any community anywhere else in the world. Not that they had become social pariahs. Not in the least. They visited any community event which still bothered to invite them in equal measure. But neither had any nerves of remote apologia or embarrassment. That was what tied them to each other.

Vikas and Zainab had a huge social circle in Zurich. As in every point in that circle knew them and they knew them. They socialised, but never internalised either the people or the parties. They knew how to have a good laugh and waltz their way through social occasions. Vikas's profession as a top private banker gave them plenty of opportunities to practise fake smiles and even faker hugs. So, they picked up the good parts and practised them in the social gatherings. It was fun. Fun to be a part, yet not to feel a part of. Fun to watch, yet not take in. They were the peripatetic onlookers of the social scene of Zurich but did not hold anything to heart. For the heart to heart, they had each other and that was more than enough. This was a bond, which could only be felt, not observed. That was the real sacredness of their relationship. The emotional purity which no one could defile.

At one point an Indian businessman who used to visit the Zurich Bollywood Ball every year from Luxembourg had told Vikas that if he could have mustered the courage, he would have done the same. Vikas smiled at Zainab who was gulping down a vodka lemonade at a distance and when their eyes met, she knew exactly what it is that the *uncleji* had said.

Vikas again never thought of justifying his actions or being a vanguard of leading the charge for men, he only smiled and told the man to still go for it! By then, the DJ was blasting a remixed version of *Teri Aankhen Jhukhi Jhukhi, Tera Chehra Khila Khila* and there is nothing more than grooving to that song with Zainab that Vikas wanted to do at that moment. And so, they did. There was nothing perfect about their moves either. They were neither in sync with each other nor in symphony with the tune. At least not Vikas. But Zainab didn't care. It was just the pure exhilaration of being together and do this.

Because that is precisely what Vikas, and Zainab had done. They had made a desperate, last- ditch attempt to stitch together their lives as best as they could. It was not perfect, nor was it free of scars. But it was the best they could have gotten in the circumstances. And they made a run for it. Without each other they would have gotten so far down the ocean, that there would have been no redemption. Now both had the zest to live. To live longer in each other's company. Again, to make up for every moment lost. Lost to time. Lost to circumstance.

Their parents perhaps would never understand, but that mattered not anymore. And this was the routine for the last several years. Not just at the Zurich Bollywood Ball, but any party which would have them, from Cologne to Luxembourg to Monaco. Any gathering, august or otherwise which would have the Managing Director of Banque Wedderburn Privee. The private banker with the biggest book of business who ever walked the streets of Zurich. And life was just starting for Vikas.

Book XII

The Twist in the Tail (2018)

1.

Utkarsh Panchal, a down on his luck Gujarat cadre Indian Revenue Service Officer suddenly received a call from the PMO to head a task force to compel foreign banks to share data and bring back sufficient amounts of money. The black variety that is.

The bad part about these down on their luck officers is that they take to any new task as if it is their chance at redemption. So, once he was given a list of names selectively pruned by the Prime Minister's Office, he set about it with a vengeance never seen before. Unlike others of his ilk who would make a beeline for the businessmen's premises and raid the life out of them, he started at the bottom. Utkarsh was convinced that raiding the businessmen would only alarm them into taking actions which would not lead to anything beneficial.

He spread out his net wide, tapped into conversations between leading chartered accountants, corporate lawyers, top *hawala* operators and started mapping out the key linkages. Some of Utkarsh Panchal's early successes involved petty bribery where businessmen in India were paying for foreign vacations of government officials in exchange for some favours or looking the other way. It didn't move the needle. He was told and therefore was steadfastly focussed on the list of names who must be brought to justice.

Somehow all the links seemed to go dry in the United Arab Emirates. Either he could spend a lot of time cultivating links there and finding the trail of money or actually start a scatter gun approach with the top Swiss banks.

He sent out notices seeking information from a whole host of Swiss banks. One such notice landed up with Jeremy Franks. He immediately understood where this was headed. Having been snubbed by the bank's management after having successfully put Vikas in the bank, this was just the opening he needed. To make a final push. To reclaim what was his.

And this was God send. He only could not figure out just yet whether to make a scapegoat of Vikas or to use him as an accomplice to draw out Mark. The slimy Mark. The one who always wriggled through howsoever narrow the exit. This time would be different promised Jeremy to himself. But the more organisational part of Jeremy also told him that this would have to a be surgical strike on Mark alone. Whatever he did could not afford to inflame Banque Wedderburn Privee.

While putting the away the letter received, he also made a mental note to ensure he spoke to legal counsel before finalising any course of action. Also, the legal counsel would only be told as much as they needed. There was no way he was handing over this letter in its entirety.

2.

Mark was furious when he learnt that Jeremy Franks had responded to some request from Indian tax authorities. He was astonished that someone in the European banking set up for so long would be so foolish as to imperil not just a bank but an entire industry.

For Mark, the letter was meant to be sent to the Swiss Banking Association for them to deliberate the next steps. This was not a request. This was an attack. Trust a bean counter like Jeremy not to pick it up. Once a bean counter, always a bean counter. And with that Jeremy was exiled to the Operations floor forever and Mark with full approval of the executive committee of the bank, never wanted to see him again.

Mark smirked in his mind's eye imaging Jeremy sitting on the Operations floor- finally defeated, finally satiated.

Mark as was his nature also assured the executive committee of the bank that he had reviewed Jeremy's response and there was nothing to be worried about in the medium term. The response did not offer much specific information, except one fatal flaw that it kind of confirmed that Banque Wedderburn Privee did hold monies from Indian origin families.

That is all Utkarsh Panchal really needed though. His intelligence systems had already confirmed the identity of the sole Indian banker there, namely Vikas Kumar. So, he just had to link it altogether. The best part of the system he was working with was that once questioned, he could reverse the onus on the hunted, rather than having to piece together everything dry. He did not have to. He would not be able, that he admitted.

Epilogue

Rishika commenced a degree program at the University of Zurich to study a bachelorette degree in psychology. Vikas and Rishika did not divorce but did not stay together either.

Zainab moved home to become the opposite number of Vikas.

Varun returned to India after his master's degree was over and started working at IIT Kanpur. Once a UP *ka bhaiyya*, always a UP *ka bhaiyya*. The most suave assistant professor in Kanpur or for that matter in any IIT anywhere in India.

Sejal gave birth to a son back home in Mahua after Prakhar's contract in Zurich was over.

Mr. and Mrs. Siddiqui left for the Hajj pilgrimage in Mecca on US passports and were accorded a royal welcome on both sides of the journey. The US passports were just too powerful for anyone to mess with.

Mr. and Mrs. Pradhan wound up their shop at *Peetal Mandi* and started planning for the Amarnath *yatra*.

Magnus Montgomery lay in blissful coma a good fifteen years after his tumble down the Alps.

Sometimes, Vikas wondered what life would have been for each of the people he encountered in these fifteen years but for that one misstep on the Alps. But, at all other times, he felt fortunate at what he had got in the bargain.

In Gratitude

This book is an amalgam of many people, cities, experiences and distinct historical episodes which have fascinated me.

Recently while speaking at my school, Vasant Valley at an event on careers in law and liberal arts, I expressed my gratitude towards Mrs. Rekha Krishnan who instilled a love for history at an early age. Moreover, together with a love for history she gave me significant opportunities to express myself through debates, writing for the school newsletter and external newspapers and magazines. Mrs. Krishnan taught me the importance of exploring current events through the lens of historical occurrences which has held me in good stead in a career in law and subsequently finance. Many aspects of this book owe their initial trajectory to what was set in motion by Mrs. Krishnan and several other teachers including Mr. Arun Kapur, Mrs. Kokila Katyal, Mrs. Tina Kishore and Mrs. Ranu Dattagupta.

I would be remiss in my duties and in serious trouble (!) if I do not thank my wife, Garima and my son, Arhaan, who gave me regular hall passes from domestic duties to focus on this book! Not to mention, Garima remains one of my harshest critics and one of the best editors ever to have walked this planet.

This book owes a debt of gratitude to several people who have always encouraged me to keep writing and in no particular order: Vikash Gupta, Richa Grover, Amlan Goswami, Naiyya Singh, Gaurav Desai, Aditi Kalra, Vijay Lakshmi Lal, Ankur Singla, Sujata Setia, Priyanka Biswas.

A special word is due for Priyanka Biswas, who designed the cover of this book soaking in every vibe of the characters and episodes to distil into what I consider an absolute work of art.

About the Author

Shayan is a gold medalist and graduate of the National Law School of India University in Bangalore. He has been writing on a wide variety of topics for several publications for the last 25 years. He blogs his writings on: saionton.wordpress.com. His first book Seven Attempts continues to receive love across continents.

He is a strategic advisor to several UHNW families, corporate groups and family offices and is also qualified to practice law in England & Wales and India.

Printed in Great Britain
by Amazon

10704666R00109